HORSE CANYON

He was an outlaw; she and her brother were innocent, stalked like prey by Frank Garn and his rangemen. Who could defend a woman and a sick man on the run? Oliver Dunhill may have been an outlaw, but he wasn't going to let a bunch of renegades hunt down unarmed and helpless people; so he bought into her troubles.

JIM SLAUGHTER

HORSE CANYON

Complete and Unabridged

LINFORD
Leicester

First published in Great Britain in 1989 by
Robert Hale Limited
London

First Linford Edition
published April 1991
by arrangement with
Robert Hale Limited London

British Library CIP Data

Slaughter, Jim *1916 –*
    Horse Canyon. — Large print ed. —
    Linford western library
    I. Title
    813.54 [F]

ISBN 0–7089–7011–7

Published by
F. A. Thorpe (Publishing) Ltd.
Anstey, Leicestershire

Set by Words & Graphics Ltd.
Anstey, Leicestershire
Printed and bound in Great Britain by
T. J. Press (Padstow) Ltd., Padstow, Cornwall

1

A Hidden Place

PHYSICALLY, the canyon was one of those isolated, spring-watered places which were deep enough to escape the bitter cold and wild winds of winter, yet broad and long enough to provide shelter, abundant feed and forage for a wide variety of wildlife.

There were trees down there, flourishing stands of thornpin thickets, grass stirrup-high for the three best seasons, spring, summer and autumn, and inevitably, some ancient mud ruins as well as at least two not-so-ancient log trapper-hunter shacks which were now in varying degrees of decay.

Geographically, Horse Canyon was sixteen miles northwest of the nearest town, which was a stockman's settlement called Paloverde and while there was clear evidence of human habitation it seemed to have a lapse of hundreds of years between the anasazi inhabitants of long ago, and the more recent log-house-builders who could have been trappers, hunters, or possibly hunted men in need of a place like Horse Canyon which was infrequently visited, but who in any case had seclusion whether they required it or not.

Except for noisy birds which made daily challenges concerning territorial rights, and the occasional cougar who screamed to either attract the opposite sex or who also established a right of domain by hair-raising racket, Horse Canyon was a quiet, peaceful, timeless place, which was how the man on the mule-nosed bay horse assessed it as he entered from the north and rode about a third of its length before making camp near the little spring-fed creek where cottonwoods were handy for hanging things, particularly items such as horse-leather impregnated with salt from sweat.

He was in his thirties, had been a

rangeman since his early teens and therefore knew perfectly well that among most wild creatures while the first instinct was mating, the second one was finding salt, either at the rare salt-lick or by eating someone's saddle-blanket, or horse-leather which had salt in it.

He was 'savvy' in other ways too. After making camp, gathering faggots for cooking-fires, he stood above the creek where his shadow sent trout minnows exploding in all directions, and having satisfied himself about a source of nearby food, he went carbine in hand on a little exploratory stroll leaving the mule-nosed bay horse hobbled in feed to its knees.

He found three things within rifleshot of his camp. The first one was a very old, crumbling, square and flat-roofed Indian jacal. It had no windows and the doorway faced eastward. Rains had grooved its walls and washed away most of the roof, but if a person did not mind sunlight and moonlight coming down upon him where the roof had once been, it was a livable structure. Small, somewhat confining with no way to see out except through the doorway or the ceiling, but livable.

The second discovery held him in place the longest. Barefoot horse tracks, dozens of them, fairly fresh and layered one above the other near the creek where paths through the bushes had been punched from several directions by thirsty animals.

He squatted there to roll a smoke and examine the 'sign'. Wild horses, many of them perhaps in three individual bands. He could guess the total number, perhaps something like a hundred of them, but except for a track here and there with an individual characteristic, he could only make one other observation; he made that from fingering the wiry limbs of the underbush where hair had clung. A lot of bay horses, but that would surprise no one since there were more bay horses in the world than any other colour.

His third discovery was made with the sun hovering above the canyon's westerly barranca. A fire-ring with fairly fresh char in it, along with cropped grass and some tree limbs worn from having been used as hangers.

A fairly recent camp, he told himself, of two individuals wearing moccasins. Possibly Indian hunters or wanderers. There were plenty of both now that the land they had once owned had been taken from them, leaving some of them to wander restlessly and aimlessly.

He spent over an hour at this place trying to piece together who those people might have been and how long ago they'd been in the canyon.

That Indians might still be around was no surprise. They'd probably known of this place since time out of mind, word of its benefits passing from generation to generation. But these two had not settled in, and that was puzzling because a place such as Horse Canyon was ideal for hold-outs; they could stay here indefinitely and, by using no more than normal precaution, be undiscovered for years because, obviously, this canyon was not only too distant from settlements to be visited very often but so far anyway, probably because it was not visible from the high, rolling grasslands above, had attracted no permanent two-legged residents.

The newcomer returned to his camp with the sun below the shielding barrancas, watched his horse crop grassheads in total contentment, then made a tiny supper-fire from hotly-burning dry twigs and unrolled his blankets, shed his hat, leaned aside the scarred old saddlegun and watched stars steadily brighten from a sickly pale colour to full-fledged diamond-brilliance.

A big cat called from the eastern rims somewhere, far enough away so that its scream lacked the usual harshness, and later, foraging owls sailed through on silent wings on their nocturnal rodent hunt.

The horseman's name was Oliver Dunhill. He had a dusting of grey at the temples, steady blue eyes, a weathered set of even features partially hidden by beard stubble, and although he was fairly tall this fact was made less noticeable by his breadth. His movements were supple and easy despite his powerful physique. He did not, at first impression, seem to be an excitable man, neither troubled nor troublesome, although his hip-holstered single-six Colt had good bluing and handsome horn grips. The rest of his attire and equipment was worn, very serviceable, shiny from many rubbings and scarred from years of use. But the gun with the horn handles looked neither old nor marked by the inevitable bumps and scratches which showed on just about everything else he owned from the seven-eighths-double rangeman's saddle with the roper's cantle and thick-throated horn, to the stained hat and scuffed cowhide boots.

Before bedding down he carefully rolled the shellbelt and placed it close by with the holster on top and the saw-handle grips toward him.

For a long while he lay listening to the mule-nosed horse picking feed. He watched the rash of high stars as he'd done many nights in solitary camps, and slept without knowing when he'd drifted off.

He awakened to the cold chill of pre-dawn, remained motionless with just his eyes moving for a long time, then sat up and reached for his boots, yawned, cleared his pipes and looked around.

The bay horse was gone.

For ten seconds the man scarcely breathed before arising to stamp into his boots and walk out yonder. The hobbles were lying in the grass, unbuckled and tossed aside. Dew showed where one set of tracks had approached and had departed leading the horse. Oliver sighed, went back to eat a cold meal, take the Winchester and strike out.

Once the sun arrived to burn the dew off there would still be bent grass to indicate the route of the horsethief, which went over toward the westerly barranca then almost straight southward.

An hour later he halted to drink at the creek before resuming his tracking.

As he wiped water from his chin he also shook his head. This was either an inexperienced horsethief or a very wily one. Inexperienced because he'd made no effort to mask his tracks. Wily, if his strategy was to use the tracks to lure Oliver into an ambush farther down the canyon. For a fact Horse Canyon had dozens of ideal bushwhacking sites.

When he left the creek he continued along the trail of his horse and tried to imagine why the thief was not astride the animal instead of in front of it leading it like an old milk cow.

Horsetheft was a killing offence, particularly in country where to set a man afoot was likely to also ensure his death. Horsethieves struck hard and afterwards rode fast.

Not this one.

When the sun finally came over the eastern barrancas with the abruptness of a seed being popped out of a grape, the brilliance was dazzling, distances became readable, and the shod-horse tracks continued as they had since before dawn to meander in an almost casual manner over along the grassy base of the westerly bluffs.

Oliver changed strategy. Since the thief had not once changed course, not even to try and confuse a tracker, he gambled that the thief would not change course, and slipped back toward the creek where he'd been shielded from detection and increased his gait, at times where this was possible, to a steady trot.

His objective was to get ahead of the horsethief. He could have trailed him, probably all day and right up into his camp after nightfall, but he wanted to end this before nightfall.

The longer he pressed the pursuit the more baffled he became. No attempt had been made to ambush him, which was something any self-respecting horsethief would have tried by now. Nor had the thief got astride and left nothing but dust in his wake, which would have been the prudent course for even a half-witted inexperienced thief, and which would also, in all possibility, have separated

Oliver Dunhill and his mule-nosed bay horse forever.

By mid-afternoon when he thought he might be far enough ahead of the horsethief to establish his own ambush, he had about come to the conclusion that he was dealing with either an idiot or, if it was an Indian, a bloody-hand, one of those totally unreasoning stronghearts who scorned any such thing as caution in the hope of enticing someone into man-to-man combat.

But if this was indeed a strongheart, then he was the first Oliver had ever heard of who would lead a horse instead of ride one.

He found a thicket full of tiny wrens whose normal existence was thrown into wildly chirping confusion by his intrusion. The birds departed, Oliver worked his way into the thicket with the westerly barranca in sight, bent aside some limbs so that his field of fire would be ample, got comfortable and was prepared to wait for the thief to come meandering along leading the mule-nosed bay horse when another inhabitant of Horse Canyon whose routine had been interrupted rattled menacingly from a distance of no more than ten feet.

It was a greenish-hided timber rattler almost as thick as a man's forearm. Any rattlesnake was deadly but timber rattlers, shorter than other rattlesnakes, were also much thicker, more venomous and also more belligerent.

This one had at least six rattles and perhaps as many as eight. It was impossible to count them when the snake was vibrating them violently.

It was said rattlesnakes could not strike farther than their length, which was logical, but no one in his right mind ever put that to a test, certainly not Oliver Dunhill who had sweat on his face and beneath his shirt as he and the snake eyed each other.

In this kind of situation a man did not move; he sat perfectly motionless for as long as was required, because all wild animals, including rattlesnakes, eventually abandoned their fighting stance; in this case, their fighting coil.

At times this could require one hell of a long time. Oliver probably could have drawn and fired his belt-gun before the snake could strike, but if he did he would alert the oncoming horsethief that he was approaching an ambush.

The rattling became intermittent. The snake's tongue flicked, his lidless eyes were fixed on the squatting man right up until some tiny animal moved to his right and he turned his head.

After that, the snake sank slowly back into his coil, rattled only slightly and indifferently and eventually came out of the coil to whip away with surprising speed until he was lost to sight among the ground-hugging shoots of the underbush.

Oliver waited a long time before lifting his hat, mopping off sweat, dropping the hat back down and twisting very slowly from the waist to find the snake.

It was gone.

He blew out a ragged breath, tipped his hat and resumed the vigil, hoping the horsethief had not passed by during his staring-session with the timber rattler.

He hadn't. Oliver heard him coming; not the thief, his steel-shod bay horse.

He mopped sweat off again, raised the Winchester, took a decent rest using one arm as a prop, and waited.

2

Strangers

H E couldn't believe it. The horsethief came into full view, visible through glass-clean air, leading Oliver's horse and concentrating on something up ahead, neither looking left nor right nor pausing to listen for pursuit.

It was a girl.

He had her brisket in both gunsights, thumb lying lightly to cock the weapon, trigger-finger curled gently inside the guard, his breath dammed stock-still in his throat.

She was young but even so his narrowed eye squinting down the barrel found unmistakable evidence that she had to be a female.

Her clothing was torn, patched, but not so ragged and loose that Oliver could not be positive she was neither a man nor a boy.

Her long hair was plaited up the back of her head. It was a glistening shade of very dark reddish auburn.

She was wearing moccasins.

Oliver lowered the saddlegun, breathed deeply a couple of times, until the shaking left his hands, and rocked back a little. If she — whoever she was — lived to be a hundred she would never come as close to being shot dead as she'd just come, and there she was, leading his horse along as she walked without haste, his horse happily, even contentedly, following like a dog, very clearly as innocent of how such things as stealing horses commonly ended as a child would have been.

He spat, shoved up to his feet, which made enough noise to bring the horse's head up and around as he stepped out of concealment and said, "That's far enough! Right where you are! If you got a weapon, don't try for it! Stand still!"

For a moment he thought she'd drop the lead-rope and run. She seemed to be as tight-wound as a spring as she watched him approach. To make her reconsider he said, "Takin' horses that don't belong to you can get you hung from a tree or maybe shot out of hand."

He stopped, grounded the Winchester and gazed at her. She was frightened, she was also no child even though there were freckles across the bridge of her nose and her mouth was soft and full. She seemed to be scarcely breathing. Oliver wagged his head.

"What's your name?"

She remained silent, big-eyed and scarcely breathing.

"Well, all right," he told her. "My name is Oliver Dunhill and that horse you're holding carried me down out of Colorado into this place, an' before that he worked stock with me as far north as Timberline, Montana. I'm fond of him. I don't take it kindly havin' someone try to steal him. Now, let's try again. What's your name?"

This time she answered. "You know my name!"

Oliver's eyes widened. He'd never set eyes on her before in his life. He leaned on the Winchester. "If I knew your name, lady, I wouldn't have asked it, would I?" He looked around then back. "Do you have a camp down here?"

Her colour was returning, it was angry red. Her terrified expression had changed into a defiant glare. She did not answer him.

Oliver tipped his hat back while studying her. He had a stirring of troubled bemusement. "All right, let's just hike on down to your camp." He hoisted the Winchester to the crook of his arm and jerked his head for her to lead the way. She stood like stone, but this time she spoke.

"I'm not going down there. If you caught me, the others'll be with — at the camp."

Oliver rolled his eyes. "What others?"

She sneered at him. "I know who you are. I know the others are with you. You

18

can't fool me, mister."

Oliver made a shrewd guess about something. "Lady, if your camp is southward, an' if there's someone down there you don't want to see, well that's fine with me. But my camp was back up north several miles an' my tracks came from even farther north. So I wouldn't be with your friends, now, would I?"

She'd been gripping the lead-rope in a sweaty white-knuckled hand. Now, she loosened the grip slightly, but that was the only indication Oliver noticed that she might be wavering in her defiance.

He smiled at her. "Who's down there?"

"Garn."

"Is that a cuss-word or a name, Lady?"

"Frank Garn and the other three. And my brother."

"Ah. Your brother."

"That's why I took your horse. We don't have horses. I smelled your supper-fire last night and came up to wait until you were asleep."

"What's that got to do with Mister Garn an' your brother?"

19

"My brother's sick but we got to keep moving, to get away from here. I thought you'd be one of Garn's riders."

Oliver frowned about that. "Is this Frank Garn huntin' for you an' your brother?"

"Yes. He's been on our trail for a long time. I've lost track. Maybe ten, fifteen days."

"Lady, if he hasn't caught up to you in that length of time chances are — "

"He stole our horses four nights back. That's how close he is. Mister, who are you? What're you doing down in this canyon?"

"I told you my name. Oliver Dunhill. I just happened onto the upper end of the canyon from up north, an' since I'm goin' nowhere in particular an' got all spring an' summer to get there, my idea was to settle in for a while an' just sort of rest, maybe hunt a little, and see if I could maybe catch some wild horses."

She seemed not quite convinced so he added a little more. "Maybe it don't make much difference, but seems to me

20

you got no choice. You can trust me, or I can take you back to my camp, tie your wrists in back and go lookin' for a town with a lawman an' hand you over for bein' a horsethief."

She blanched, stood in silence for a moment then let her shoulders droop. Oliver thought she was really quite pretty, or would be if she was cleaned up and dressed in something besides rags.

"Leave the horse here," she told him, and moved toward a young tree to tie the animal. He watched her with dispassionate interest. She moved purposefully, like someone who, having made up her mind, would now pursue a goal. As she faced him she said, "Be quiet. Just follow along."

He nodded, let her take the lead and with the Winchester in the crook of one arm, trailed after her. She was not meandering now, her stride was long and forceful.

It wasn't a very long walk, which suited Oliver just fine. Since childhood he'd been of the opinion that the reason

God, or someone anyway, had given horses a small brain and four legs, and a man a larger brain and two legs, was because he intended that the horse should do the walking for the man.

Where she finally halted he could detect the faint scent of woodsmoke, but directly ahead was a dense thicket and several shaggy old large trees. She turned and looked at him. "My brother's name is Walt. He's been failing for the past three or four days."

"What's wrong with him?"

"I don't know. He's sort of listless an' weak. Let me walk in front. He's got a gun."

Oliver jutted his jaw. "Go ahead."

Their camp was in the middle of the thicket; except for the woodsmoke scent and human movement, it would have been hard to detect.

An old saddleboot with a Winchester butt protruding from the top was hanging from a low tree-limb. There were two soiled bedrolls and some saddlebags, otherwise it was a Spartan camp.

The man lying on his side fast asleep looked a little like the girl, same colour hair, same good features, but drawn and tired-looking. Oliver, who could mouth a horse for age and come shrewdly close to guessing a man's age, thought the sleeping man was in his thirties. About the girl he did not even try to guess.

He followed her. When she knelt to reach for a canteen before awakening the sweating, drawn and haggard-looking man, she spoke over her shoulder to Oliver. "He was worse yesterday and don't seem any better today."

The man awakened, looked dully at his sister, looked past at the thick, stubbly-faced armed man behind her and rasped out a curse and tried to hoist himself into a sitting position, but the girl held him down as she spoke. "He's not one of them. I stole his horse last night to fetch down here for you. He caught me. His name's Oliver Dunhill."

The man finally sat up. His shirtfront was dark with sweat and his eyes were not only sunken, but seemed to focus only intermittently, like someone with a high fever.

Oliver slowly knelt to lean on his carbine. He had a pony of brandy back in his saddlebags but it wouldn't help here. He told the man his name, repeated what he'd told the girl, then said, "By any chance did you get snake-bit, or maybe hit by a scorpion? You sure as hell got poisoned some way, friend."

The younger man ignored that and looked questioningly at the girl. She shrugged. "I'm taking him at his word, Walt. I can't do anything else."

The man turned his feverish, troubled glance back to Dunhill. "You can't do us any good, mister. They're just over the horizon by now."

Oliver smiled about that. "Maybe. Can you hold onto a horse's mane?"

"Why? Where's the horse?"

"Tied to a tree back yonder. Can you hold on long enough to ride a couple miles?"

The girl stood up. In her quick manner she said she'd go get the horse. After she'd departed Oliver got comfortable on the ground. "I was just passin' through. Goin' no place in particular."

The younger man eyed Oliver dolefully. "You better keep right on riding, then, because if they catch you with us, mister — "

"We'll talk about that up at my camp. I got some brandy up there. You look like a man who needs to have some, then to keep covered and sweat like hell for a day or so." Oliver paused, looked up where the girl had disappeared and asked a question. "Why is this Frank Garn after you?"

"You better ride on, mister."

"Yeah, I probably should, but your wife — "

"My sister. Annabelle."

"All right, your sister Annabelle tried to steal my horse. That gives me at least a toehold in this mess, so just tell me straight out: why is Garn after you folks?"

"Because we got somethin' he's got to have."

"Money?"

"No. A deed to a piece of land southwest of here a hell of a long ride."

"His deed? You stole the deed to his land?"

"No. It's the deed to land our uncle left us when he died last year. Garn was his superintendent. When Annabelle an' I showed up a month or so back to claim the land by reason of inheritance, Garn was already living in my uncle's house an' sellin' cattle, horses, even some of the land, like he owned everything."

"How long had Garn worked for your uncle?"

"Thirteen years, that's what made him think he should own everything. If he can get the deed and burn it . . . As long as we have it, mister, he's got to bust every law in the world to catch us an' get it."

"How'd you happen to have the deed?"

"My uncle mailed it to us back in Missouri along with his will."

"Garn knew about this will an' deed?"

"Sure. We showed them both to him."

"Didn't he try to get them when you did that?"

"Yes. We got away by the skin of our teeth an' been running ever since. An' right now I'd give him the damned deed. If he rode in here right now I'd . . . He'll kill us both, mister."

The girl arrived leading Oliver's horse. Rounding up their meagre belongings did not take long, nor did it take long to boost the ill man onto the horse for the girl to lead back the way she'd come earlier.

Oliver walked in the rear, with his Winchester, studying them both and pondering what the younger man had told him. By the time they were approaching his camp the sun was sinking, there were shadows on the west side of the barrancas, and a covey of plump little topknotted valley quail whose members had been foraging the camp, made a noisy exit by flinging high into the air and beating a retreat in all directions.

Oliver was tired from walking. The

girl and the horse seemed the least tired as they got the younger man into a sheltered place where Oliver gave him three swallows from his little pony of brandy, covered him until he resembled a mummy, then went with the girl to make a supper-fire.

As she worked he smoked and watched, spat aside a couple of times and finally, when she handed him a dented tin cup of hot coffee, asked her the same question he'd asked several times before.

"What is your name?"

She answered without even a pause. "Annabelle Lee. I already told you my brother's name. Walt Lee. The man he told you about, our uncle, was named Henry Lee." She sat on the ground looking at him. "If I had a ton of pure gold I'd give it to you for the horse."

He sipped hot java and smiled at her. "It'd take just about that much. He's an old friend of mine. Annabelle, one horse wouldn't help a lot. You need two horses."

"What we need is a doctor, the

protection of the law, and if we can't get those things, a long head-start so we can get out of New Mexico. And never come back."

"And lose all that land?"

"Mister Dunhill, it's a big ranch, worth a lot of money. There are four steady riders and they are all four of them hunting us right this minute. My uncle ran a lot of livestock. Do you know what I'd cheerfully do right this minute if Frank Garn rode in here?"

Oliver knew. "Give him the works if he'd help you get your brother to a settlement where there's a doctor. Thing is, Annabelle, if Frank Garn's been after you for close to three weeks, he's not trying to catch up to make a deal with you. My guess is that he'll take your papers and bury the pair of you."

3

In Peril

THE Lees were exhausted, probably as much from anxiety and sleepless nights as from their exertions the day before, but whatever the reasons when Oliver silently rolled out the next morning, pulled on his boots, buckled the shellbelt and Colt into place and went over to stir shavings into last night's coals, they were both still soundly sleeping.

He got a little smokeless fire going, put the pan of coffee on to boil, took his carbine and walked eastward through dew and dawn-chill. When the sun arrived its brilliance would strike the lower side of the westward cliff-face. He did not want to be in sunshine when he got atop the rim, nor was he although it was a long walk — for someone who did not cherish hiking it was a very long walk — but he found a game-trail and went to the easterly top-out where shadows lay like grey fog over the countryside.

What he was looking for was not immediately visible but with the advent of first light it was: a distant spindrift of grey smoke from someone's breakfast-fire.

If the men around that fire were who he thought they might be, someone's guess that they were over the horizon was wrong as hell. They were more nearly at the southernmost lift of Horse Canyon, and that was not even close to the horizon.

He squatted in dazzling newday light, built and lit a smoke for breakfast, and watched. When the smoke eventually diminished he stubbed out his cigarette, spat at a sluggish lizard for whom the heat had as yet not warmed his working parts, and looked back down into the canyon. There was no rising smoke, but there wouldn't have been anyway;

the pile of faggots he'd left near the fire-ring consisted of only bone-dry, long-dead wood, which was smokeless unless it got wet, and his impression of this country was that it hadn't rained in a long time.

He saw a long-legged rabbit hopping from one low growth of scrub brush to another, nibbling a little at each bush. He could have shot it for meat but didn't. In open, flat country like the plateau above Horse Canyon, the sound of a gunshot would travel for one hell of a distance. Anyway, there were plenty of trout in the little creek.

For the first — and last — time after encountering the fugitives named Lee he considered his own interest which, very simply, was not to get involved in the troubles of others, especially when there were four or five hard-riders pursuing them, and the best he could hope for from the fugitives was damned little practical support when push came to shove.

On the other hand, while he was no knight-errant and didn't even know what a knight-errant was, it stuck in his craw that, providing the Lees had told him the truth, in this part of the world they qualified as greenhorns and he wasn't one, hadn't ever been a greenhorn, and with the man ill and the girl busting her heart to protect her brother, they needed his help and — what the hell — this riding season he hadn't planned on doing anything, anyway.

He went back down into the canyon, reached camp as the girl was cleaning up, knelt beside Walt Lee's bedroll and was met by a vague smile. "Weak as a kitten," the younger man told him. "But I slept like a log. That brandy sure helped, Mister Dunhill."

Oliver nodded about that. "Good. It was a guess based on a little experience with fevers. Sweat it out and get lots of rest, an' drink water every time you open your eyes . . . My name is Oliver not Mister Dunhill."

The girl came over and smiled shyly at Oliver. She had some fried cornmeal if he was hungry. He smiled back as he arose to accompany her back to the fire-ring. Fried cornmeal was his idea of something unfit for a human stomach but he ate it, masked the taste with coffee, and afterwards while rolling a smoke asked Annabelle about her parents.

They were both dead, she told him. Her only living relative had been her uncle, Henry Lee. Oliver considered the glow of his quirley. "Those gents you said were south somewhere." He inhaled, exhaled and looked directly at her. "I saw a cooking-fire down near the end of Horse Canyon."

Her eyes widened slightly. He shrugged. "Maybe, maybe not. I want you to stay in camp with your brother. Don't shoot any game. There's fish in the creek, maybe you could catch a mess for supper. I'll be back maybe this evening. Tell me something: are these gents who're shagging you riding ranch horses?"

"Yes."

"What's the brand?"

"My uncle's initials back to back. HL. Mister Dunhill, there are four of them.

They're hard men. I think if we just let Walt rest one more day then struck out . . . "

He gazed wintrily at her. "We might not have one more day. Otherwise, with just one horse how do we strike out? I can't fly an' you don't have wings either." He arose, nodded to her and went out to his horse.

When he was ready to mount she came out to him. It was hard to compare the Annabelle Lee of today with the spitfire of yesterday. She said, "I feel terrible about dragging you into our troubles."

He nodded gravely about that. "It'd be a lot nicer if the three of us could spend the summer down here fishin', huntin' a little and storin' up fat for winter. But we can't." He swung up, evened the reins and gazed down at her. "I know better'n to ask personal questions, but — how old are you?"

"Twenty. Well, I'll be twenty in two months."

He had thought she was no more than about eighteen. As he smiled and reined away she called after him, "Be careful."

He raised a hand in a casual wave and set his course southward. Being careful was his nature. He'd lived a life of danger and was still above ground because he'd been careful. Prudent would have been a better description. Prudent, and shrewd.

By the time he passed the thicket where the Lees had camped the sun was soaring above Horse Canyon. Two hours later, with the sun off centre, the canyon full of boxed-in springtime heat, man and horse sweating as they sashayed southward staying in speckled shade or solid undergrowth to conceal their passage, it was possible to occasionally catch sight of the far southern lift of the canyon where it gradually rose to meet the surrounding open country.

Down here, Oliver became increasingly wary, but as long as he saw wild animals and heard birds up ahead, he remained unworried. But when there was no longer birdsong and almost no sightings of feeding varmints, he slackened to a slow walk and occasionally halted to listen.

He was something like five miles southward, sitting his horse like a statue hidden by dense tree-shade, when a flight of raffish crows took to the air up ahead a fair distance, flinging in all directions and noisily complaining about whatever it was that had disturbed them.

Oliver stepped to the ground, rolled and lit a smoke and watched the birds until they, and their noise, were distant, then he tied the horse, killed the smoke, took his saddlegun and started to scout alongside the little creek keeping well into the undergrowth as he moved along.

It was uncomfortable going. Aside from thorny bushes, low, wiry limbs and hordes of gnats and mosquitoes, he knew for a fact that Horse Canyon had snakes. He saw none but he watched for them right up until he heard a horse noisily blow its nose not too far ahead.

It did not occur to him that whoever was down there might not be a man named Frank Garn and three other riders. He'd never been this far south before; his attention was on both his surroundings and that nose-blowing horse, nothing else, and if he'd crept up on a band of Indians or commonplace mustangers he would have been greatly surprised. But no such encounters occurred right up to the moment he saw hobbled horses in a grassy clearing beside the creek. There were four of them, muscled up and ridden down to bone and steel hardness. The ones he could see best had a left shoulder brand. HL.

That was all the confirmation he required. As for the riders, he heard some desultory conversation, the words made indistinguishable by distance, but caught no sight of the speakers as he began a slow withdrawal back to the place where he'd tethered the mule-nosed bay.

They were resting, which was understandable since the breakfast smoke he'd seen much earlier had been at least six or eight miles farther south.

He drank at the creek, watered his horse, led it back a short distance then swung up over leather heading west in the direction of the barranca-face over there which was just now beginning to be shaded along its broad, nearly vertical front.

Garn would find his tracks and probably the moccasin tracks of the Lees as well. He would trace the footprints to the camp the Lees had made in the thicket. After that things would become more complicated. He would find shod-horse signs, Oliver's boot-tracks, and after puzzling over these things he would inevitably abandon speculation in favour of the practical course, which would be to follow the tracks of a horse being led northward by someone wearing moccasins and followed by someone wearing a rangeman's boots.

Oliver's reason for making a fresh set of shod-horse marks going west was to encourage the trackers to speculate that there might be two shod horses, meaning two riders instead of one. His idea was to encourage Garn to send a man, maybe two men, over the freshest shod-horse sign.

Anything he could accomplish to split up the pursuers, to confuse them, would provide a delay, and right now he wanted that more than anything else. He had to reach his camp before Garn got close. Exactly what he would do when he got back there was unclear. For the moment he wanted to slow the pursuit, confuse it if he could, and gain time.

While riding he considered, and discarded, a number of options. By the time shadows were settling into the late day when he was fairly close to the camp, he had hit upon a very chancy ruse which, if it failed, would probably get them all killed. If it succeeded, it would still not get them out of the woods but it would certainly disrupt the hell out of the pursuit.

Annabelle heard him coming long before he saw her standing beside a tree in shadowy gloom with her brother's old carbine. He smiled to himself. He had no idea how good a man Walt was, but unless he was an outstanding individual Oliver would prefer the girl's company in a tight squeeze.

He raised a hand, palm forward, and rode up into her shadowy place before halting, bracing both hands atop the saddlehorn and speaking. "They're coming. Back about where your camp was. Four of them like you said with that HL brand on their animals."

"Did you see them?"

"No ma'm. Just the horses." He swung to the ground and flung the stirrup over his saddleseat as he tugged the latigo loose and looped it through the rigging ring. "How's your brother?"

"Not as good as he thinks he is, but much better." She fell in beside him as he led the horse closer to camp before dumping the rig in the grass. "He drank some of your brandy. His colour is much better."

"Yeah," Oliver conceded drily. "It'll do that." He faced her. "They got to quit soon. You can't track folks after sundown."

"How close?"

He considered her. His experience

with women was not extensive but the few he had known had thought like females. This one thought like a man and asked questions or made statements like a man. "Close enough for us to eat a cold supper tonight and keep watch."

She said, "I caught eight trout," meaning if they could not have a fire tonight they'd miss a good meal. He walked with her over where Walt Lee was sitting with a blanket around his shoulders like an old bronco Indian. When Oliver hunkered to tell the younger man the same things he'd told the girl, Walt sat hunched in long silence, watched Oliver build a smoke and light it, then spoke.

"They were bound to overhaul us, Mister Dunhill."

"Oliver. Just plain Oliver. I expect you're right. But maybe we got more of an advantage than they got. We know they're down there an' while they know you folks, or someone anyway, is up here somewhere, as long as they can't pick up any cookin'-fire smoke or hear us, they got no idea how far ahead we are."

Annabelle returned and sat down with them as Oliver said, "I think after dark I'll go down there an' pay 'em a little visit."

Both Lees looked at him. Oliver trickled smoke past eyes narrowed in speculative thought, and when the silence had drawn out about as far as it would stretch, he said, "How would you folks handle this back in Missouri?"

Walt would have answered but his sister cut him off. "Sneak away in the night, try to find a settlement with a lawman in it."

Oliver killed his cigarette against the ground. "That'd be one way, for a fact," he told them, and raised his head. "But if there's a settlement with a lawman in it, it's not close or I'd have seen signs of it over the last couple of days. As for sneakin' away. Not with two of us on foot and them four on horseback. Once we got out of this canyon onto flat, open land, they'd run us down like devils after a bunch of crippled saints."

One thing in particular had impressed Annabelle about Oliver Dunhill since her first encounter with him: he was not an excitable individual. "Do you have a plan?" she asked, and got back one of his easy smiles when he replied.

"Yes'm, but in a situation like this even a real good plan likely won't be good enough." Oliver unwound up off the ground, sniffed the air and studied the feeble stars in their light cobalt setting. "We can't do much until it's plumb dark," he said, looking down at them. "Annabelle, you go back out yonder under that tree with the carbine. Just stand there and listen. Don't use the gun unless you got 'em so close you can see their Adam's apples. Walt, you any good at praying?"

Both the younger people sat in expressionless silence looking at the older man, who smiled at Walt. "Stay right where you are, keep covered an' warm, an' pray like hell."

Annabelle had one question. "And you, Oliver?"

"I'm goin' to shed my spurs, take just my handgun, and see if I can sneak down there where they hobbled their horses. If the Good Lord is with me an' my scent isn't too stout to carry very far, I'm goin' to do my damndest to set them afoot, an' if my luck is extra good, bring back two horses with me."

4

Toward Midnight

LUCK was fickle, so was nightfall-darkness if a man did not pay attention to its cycles. Before Oliver got down where there was a faint, ground-hugging glow of cooking-coals, a huge moon appeared at his back.

He left the bay horse in a manzanita thicket tethered to a blood-red limb thicker than a man's arm and left the carbine in its boot before he began his stalk.

He had as much of the night as he might need, but moonlight-brilliance didn't help as he began his nearly soundless search for saddle animals.

When he finally found them, hobbled and grazing, there were two horses, not four, and that kept him squatting in a thicket for a while, until he thought the other two animals might be hobbled close by but elsewhere and arose to begin a wide encircling stalk of the place where men's voices indicated the camp was.

He did not see it until he was on the east side of the place of lively small red coals. There were two men sitting there, hunched like Indians, eating and drinking coffee.

Oliver found some good background and sat down in front of it to watch the distant rangemen. Where in the hell were the other two?

There were several places they could be. He naturally thought first that they might be scouting northward, might even have found the Lees up there. It only occurred to him when he heard riders coming in from the west that his ruse farther south and much earlier had worked; the two late-arrivals had been following his shodhorse sign over along the base of the westerly cliff.

Both seated men arose and went out where the newcomers were off-saddling. It wasn't hard to see the four of them under that huge and brilliant moon, but he could only pick up a scrap of their conversation until the four returned to the low fire and sat down; then, as the hungry men went to work on a meal and hot coffee, Oliver heard what they said very clearly, and just as clearly they were disgruntled because, while they'd been able to follow the shod-horse sign without difficulty, after dusk they had to give it up even though they knew the tracks were still going northward.

What they had come back with was not an answer to the question that worried the other two men, one of whom had a gruff, throaty voice and unkempt grey hair which even his hat had been unable to press into any kind of order. He said, "Whoever he is, sure as hell he come onto Walt an' the girl."

No one denied this. It seemed reasonably obvious. But one of the late arrivals, a lanky, lean man, spoke around a mouthful of food to say "Frank; there ain't supposed to be but them two. It's beginning to look to Andy an' me like

48

this canyon's got other folks in it."

The man with the awry hair answered bluntly "If it has, that's not goin' to make no difference. If we run onto them, let 'em wonder all they want. I'd say a place like this — if it's got anyone livin' in it — would be a real fine place for renegades to hide out. Sure as hell even homesteaders would have better sense'n to settle in here." The gruff-voiced man flung coffee-grounds in Oliver's direction and fumbled for the makings as his companions muttered among themselves.

Oliver's impression was that at least that lone lanky man was wearying of this unrewarding pursuit. Maybe the others also were, but that man who was lighting his smoke had the look and sound of someone who would track a fly across a mile of glass windows and never even think of giving up. Oliver also thought he would be Frank Garn.

He was right. About the time Oliver had heard enough and was preparing to arise, fade farther back and begin his big, circling sashay around where the horses were, a voice Oliver had not heard before, and which was slow with a hint of a Texas drawl, said, "Frank, back home the cattle will have drifted all over the countryside."

If that was meant as an admonition, Garn reacted to it bluntly. "We can get 'em back, but right now I want that feller an' his sister."

The same faintly drawling voice said, "Yeah, hasn't been no question about that for a long time. What sticks in my craw is — why?"

Garn snarled his reply. "I told you fellers when we struck out, them two stole some legal papers that belonged to old Henry an' unless I get 'em back they can use 'em to claim the ranch an' fire all of us."

Whether this satisfied the three rangemen or not was not made clear, but one thing had been made clear, Frank Garn's temper had been aroused and to Oliver, who was still watching and listening, it seemed clear that none of the riders wanted to push Garn any farther.

Oliver slipped back through underbush to begin his long sashay around where the horses were cropping grass in a small glade west of the creek.

The moon had soared. Instead of its original faint egg-yolk colour, it was now almost pure white, its glow brightening the night almost to daytime brilliance.

He made good time even though he had to go far out and around before edging up close to the little clearing. The horses did not detect his presence until he hunkered in one place studying them, then they raised their heads, pointed their ears, and gazed in his direction, but went right on chewing. They knew he was over there but were not very concerned.

He waited a long time. There was no way to reach the animals without walking away from all cover. He thought the men at the campfire would perhaps make one final inspection before turning in, but since they'd been talking when he'd left he assumed they would still be doing that, would not roll in for a while yet and therefore would not make a final round of the camp for possibly another hour or so.

He was wrong.

Two of the horses were bays, one was line-backed grulla and the fourth animal was powerfully put-together dark sorrel with a roached mane; he was probably someone's working stockhorse. Men who roped from the back of horses commonly roached manes so there would be no flowing long hair to interfere with their roping.

Oliver arose and that of course was noticed by the animals, but as before, they looked in his direction briefly then went back to eating. If he'd smelled like an Indian their reaction would probably have been very different, but one rangeman smelled pretty much like other rangemen.

He walked slowly, allowing the horses time to become accustomed to his presence. They watched but at first made no attempt to hop away. When that happened only the grulla horse came around on his hind legs, planted both hobbled front legs flat down and began hopping.

Oliver halted.

The other horses alternately eyed the timid grulla and the stationary man, decided not to go with the grulla and went back to grazing. The grulla, for whatever reason, stopped hopping, probably because his four-legged companions did not share his anxiety. But he stayed slightly apart as Oliver resumed his approach.

He was completely visible out there. The nearest concealing undergrowth was several hundred feet distant, but if he could get in among the horses they would provide cover. He finally began to soothingly talk, something which evidently worked because the three horses grazing together ignored him as they swung their heads to reach farther for grass without having to hop to get it.

Oliver got to within fifteen feet of the handsome sorrel horse, saw the back-to-back shoulder brand, leaned from the hips to locate the hobbles in the grass, and one of the bay horses actually made several little crop-hops closer to examine Oliver as he was studying the hobbles.

The sorrel horse was hobbled with a finely made set of plaited rawhide, doubled hobbles without buckles. They were held closed by a large rawhide button, half the size of a silver dollar, which had been forced through two rawhide loops.

The two bays had ordinary chain hobbles with large harness buckles. When they moved the short length of chain between each hobble rattled, but not very loudly.

He did not bother with the spooky grulla horse. He would like to chouse all four of them away but he'd settle for three if the fourth one proved troublesome. He had already made up his mind to take the friendly bay and the husky sorrel as he chummed his way right up to the sorrel, gently touched its shoulder, and as the horse raised its head from the ground Oliver ran his hand from the shoulder down the animal's leg to the fetlock so the horse would know where his hand was at all times.

He sank to one knee and began working those large rawhide buttons through their double loops. It was a hell of a job. Somewhere along the line the hobbles had gotten wet. The rawhide had swelled. Reluctantly, because he admired the rawhide hobbles, Oliver dug out his clasp-knife, cut the loops on one hobble and was leaning to do the same on the far side when all four horses flung up their heads.

Oliver felt the sorrel horse tense. He remained on his knees, twisted to look rearward, and saw the tall silhouette approaching past the underbush from the direction of the camp. So far the man had not seen him but that was at best a temporary situation.

Oliver crawled around to the far side of the sorrel horse, tugged loose the tie-down over his beltgun hoped as hard as he could that the rangeman would not come all the way out to the horses, and saw no evidence that the man's final round before turning in would be that cursory, and got up into low crouch with the sorrel between them, drew his sixgun and waited.

The tall man bypassed all three horses, and Oliver, to go back where the grulla horse began gathering himself to hop away from the approaching tall man.

He spoke quietly to the horse as he continued toward him. "Blue, just stand easy, no one's goin' to hurt you." Maybe the grulla knew the man but that seemed to make no difference, he continued to edge away. A spooky horse was a spooky horse as long as he lived. Some would learn to tolerate one individual but evidently this horse was not one of those because as the man got close enough to raise his arm slowly, the horse hopped a short distance before stopping, softly snorting and rolling his eyes.

The lanky man dropped his arm and

swore. This time he ran at the horse, and this time although the horse tried hard to get clear, he was unable to. The man caught him by the mane, yanked his head around and swore at him, which did not help any but at least the horse had been caught.

The tall man evidently had very little patience and a fierce temper. He swung his fist, caught the horse alongside the nose and as the horse tried to hop away the man yanked his head around. "If you wasn't the only way I was goin' to get around up here I'd shoot you an' let the buzzards have a feast, you ugly claybank, roman-nosed cow-hocked miserable son of a bitch!"

The horse was shivering with fear, unable to do much about it until the man turned with a contemptuous oath and started back the way he had come.

And saw Oliver.

The grulla hopped farther from the man. That was the only sound as the men faced each other from a distance of about thirty feet. Oliver slowly raised his handgun navel-high, and cocked it.

The tall man seemed not to be breathing.

Oliver spoke. "Hands straight out front an' turn around."

The tall man obeyed. Oliver went up, disarmed him from behind, flung the Colt away and raised his left hand to the man's shoulder to bring his back around.

The tall man came around swinging. His bony fist caught Oliver high on the right cheek. His left fist sank into Oliver's soft parts. He also brought up a knee and the tall man was very fast. Fortunately he lacked power otherwise Oliver would have been put flat down.

He gave ground, continued to give it as the tall man rushed him to try and finish things before Oliver pulled the trigger. He never did pull it but he eased the hammer down with his thumb, swung the gun like a club, felt the shock all the way to his shoulder as steel ground into flesh and bone, and stepped back as the tall man staggered, instinctively covered his upper body with both arms and shuffled first one way then another way to gain time for recovering from the blow that had made him see dozens of tiny multi-coloured lights.

Oliver leathered the gun, went after the tall man who was still dazed, hammered him to his knees then brought up a leg to smash into the beaten man's jaw from the underside and kicked free as the tall man tried feebly to grab Oliver's legs for support, before crumpling to the ground.

Oliver's face felt feverish, his middle hurt, and as he leaned down to flop the tall man over onto his back, he saw blood from the man's mouth up across his cheek almost to the eye.

Without another look Oliver went back to the sorrel, dropped low, cut the rawhide loops, stood up to fashion a short lead from the ruined hobbles and took the sorrel with him as he freed the pair of bays, made the same kind of lead out of one other set of hobbles, and approached the grulla using his two-led horses as cover.

But it didn't work. It might have an hour earlier before the tall man had struck the grulla, but not now. He could hop with hobbles about as fast as a man could run. Oliver was in no shape to chase him so he turned northward with the two led-horses and did not even look back until he was up where his mule-nosed horse was dozing.

On the ride back leading two horses Oliver had no illusions about one thing: when that tall man was able to stagger or crawl back to camp the effect would be as though Oliver had kicked a hornet's nest.

Garn still had one horse. He would also be able to figure out that whoever had attacked the tall man and had stolen two horses had gone north and even with three men on foot — unless they could catch that other freed bay horse, in which case two men would be astride — the horsethief could not be very far ahead.

Darkness would help Oliver under normal circumstances, but this particular night it was almost as bright out as daytime. Oliver and the Lees had, he guessed, maybe half an hour, maybe a little more, to lose their pursuers, which was not the way he had planned it, but he had at least accomplished part of what he'd set out to do, and under the circumstances had to be satisfied with that.

When the three of them fled now they would be a-horseback.

5

The Elegant Gun

ANNABELLE was waiting, carbine leaning against the old tree. When he came up leading two horses she smiled so widely he thought her face would split. No mention was made of saddles or bridles as she helped him tie the animals then moved out of tree-gloom and saw his face.

He passed it off as they trudged over where her brother was waiting, wrapped like an old Pima squaw. He too noticed the swollen, discoloured side of Oliver's face, but unlike his sister did not mention it as Oliver told them they had to roll their blankets, round up their things and move out.

Walt shed the blanket and stood up as though he were not still weak. He moved swiftly. Both the Lees were efficient in their haste, which pleased Oliver. He'd told them they had an hour to get clear, at the most, and that was a strong enough incentive.

He did something that pained him to do; he cut his lariat to fashion a pair of squaw bridles for the stolen horses, helped them both aboard and handed up their bundles, coiled what remained of his rope, mounted the mule-nosed horse and led off without a word, heading northeastward in the direction of that game-trail he'd used shortly before sun-up to climb out of Horse Canyon.

As soon as it was light enough to see, Garn would pick up their tracks. As Oliver told them, there was probably enough time, about three or four hours, for them to get out of the canyon, up where the land was flat enough to permit them to make good time, before Garn could find them.

Going up that game-trail even in moonlight was a hair-raising experience. Prudent riders would have led the animals up. The trail was good and it meandered so that at no time were they climbing straight up, but it was narrow. Parts of its outer edge crumbled as the horses climbed, but eventually they reached the top-out — and got a surprise. There hadn't been a breath of air stirring down in the canyon but atop it in open country the wind was blowing, cold as a witch's bosom and steady. It was coming from the north. By instinct their animals turned their rumps to it and walked southward, which suited Oliver. He preferred having wind at his back, and otherwise it didn't make a hell of a lot of difference which direction they rode in as long as they put as many miles as possible between themselves and the men down in the canyon who would track them as soon as first light appeared.

Annabelle rode stirrup with her brother, forcing him to bundle up in a blanket. Oliver looked back once, heard them arguing, knew the girl would win, and faced forward studying as much of the grassland as he could see by moonlight.

Below somewhere, in Horse Canyon, Frank Garn and his dismounted riders would be grumbling to high heaven. That brought a tight little smile to Dunhill's craggy features.

The wind did not diminish nor increase, it blew steadily and unrelentingly, keeping the horses hiking right along, tails tucked, heads down.

They rode without a stop for two solid hours. Oliver would have suggested a lope if the Lees hadn't been balancing their gatherings precariously on horses being ridden bareback. Even so, he felt reasonably safe. Even if Garn had caught that other bay horse, only he and one other man would be able to push the pursuit. The men on foot wouldn't be any threat unless Garn could halt the flight of the people he was chasing long enough for his two men on foot to come up, and that wasn't likely to happen.

The cold increased the closer it got to daybreak. This was how Oliver estimated the time. When he could make out a distant bosque of oaks and altered course just enough to reach them, his intention was to halt for a spell, rest the horses, see how Walt was making out, and, if necessary, figure something out about the loose load each of the Lees was burdened with. His heart rose into his throat when, still a mile from the oaks, a large group of horses burst out in a flinging wild rush. Until Oliver could see them well enough to make out that they were riderless, he'd thought sure as hell they were about to be attacked by either hold-outs or renegades.

It was a band of mustangs who had evidently elected to bed down among the trees for relief from the wind as well as sheltering protection.

They had either seen or heard the oncoming riders and within minutes of breaking out of the oaks were scattering in ten different directions. Their flight was so abrupt and swift that Oliver, who was interested in wild horses, did not get a chance to look them over.

The broke horses threw up their heads and faltered their leads as they watched the wild animals, otherwise they went along until they were among the same oaks and were allowed to halt where wild-horse scent was strong. Oliver swung to the ground, a mite stiff from the cold, turned back to help Annabelle down, and the pair of them went back to take Walt's burden first, then wait for him to slide to the ground.

Oliver had his set of hobbles. There were none for the stolen horses so the three of them drifted with the animals as they sought something to fill their guts with. They talked as they were pulled along. Oliver thought they just might have got plumb clear but, if they hadn't, if they saw pursuers on their backtrail when daylight returned, providing it wasn't all four of them, it was his opinion that this protective place was probably as good as anything they might encounter farther along for people to make a stand in.

Annabelle worried about her brother, and in fact Walt did appear a little wobbly, but he seemed to Oliver to be irritated by his sister's fussing.

They chewed jerky, bundled against the cold, went with the horses in search of graze or browse, and were still doing this when Oliver waved toward the east where a sickly streak of diluted pink shone faintly above the curve of the world. "Hour more," he told them, and squatted as he gazed at the Lees. "They'll track us here," he told them. "Or, with maybe another hour of poor visibility we could get another five or six miles down-country. Maybe see rooftops or something." He left it hanging.

Walt sat down with a blanket around him. His sister had their old Winchester to lean on as she looked first at her brother then at Oliver. When neither of the men seemed inclined to speak, she said, "We have cover here. Five or six miles across more open country may take us where there is no shelter."

Oliver smiled at her but spoke to her brother. "Walt . . . ?"

"It was goin' to end up in a dog-fight sooner or later anyway. At least in this place we got shelter, they got to come at us across open country, an' we got you," the younger man replied. "Oliver, I've been wondering about something." He jutted his jaw. "That fancy gun you wear. I've seen lots of men wearing guns but darned few armed like you are. That weapon must have cost a fortune."

Oliver sat down with the reins under him, went to work rolling a smoke and said nothing until he'd fired up. It was gloomy among the oaks, windy and still cold. He trickled smoke without gazing at either of his companions. "It cost someone a fortune," he told them, "but not me."

Walt's eyes widened. "Must have been a hell of a poker session for someone to put a weapon like that in the pot."

Oliver's gaze drifted slowly to the younger man's face in the shadows. "Wasn't a poker game," he said.

"Dice, then," exclaimed Walt. "Big-stake dice game."

Oliver continued to gaze at the younger man then he shook his head. "Nope." He then would have changed the subject but Annabelle said, "I wouldn't have thought you'd be a dedicated gambler, Oliver."

He grinned at her. "What would you call it tonight, me sneakin' down there to get two more horses?"

She smiled back at him. "That's what I meant. I wouldn't have thought you'd gamble with cards or dice. If you took chances at all it'd have to be for something more serious than a card-game."

His smile faded slowly as he studied her face. Finally, he sighed and stood up. "Annabelle, you'n your brother get some rest. I'm goin' out yonder an' watch for 'em. I mean it; get some rest because I got a feelin' that when we finally leave this place you're goin' to need all the strength you got."

He left them with the horses and strolled back to the first tier of oaks where he could see in all directions except westerly, made and lit another smoke and leaned on an old tree.

The world was usually quietest just before dawn. The busy creatures who hunted or fed by night were back in their dens preparing to sleep throughout the daylight hours. It had always intrigued Oliver that nocturnal critters knew when dawn was coming even though the world was still fully dark.

By rights he should have been a hundred miles farther along. Whatever fate sat on a man's shoulder sure had one hell of a unique sense of humour. It'd let him start out to do something, then, just to prove it existed and was more powerful than the man, it turned whatever he was embarked upon into something else.

"Oliver."

He turned. She was wraithlike in the oak-gloom, holding her blanket tightly in front as she looked at him. He scowled, which was lost in the poor light. "I told you to get some rest, girl. You need it."

"So do you. I came out to spell you off."

"I don't need any spellin' off, but thanks all the same."

"Can you see anything out there?"

71

"No. But dawn'll break directly. Then they ought to be visible." He suddenly thought of something and considered her less irritably. "Which one of you's got that legal deed an' the will?"

"Neither one of us," she told him, and at his widening stare she explained. "Back at that camp where you found us; we knew they'd overtake us there. Walt was feverish and I was just about worn out. We dug in the dirt, made a rocked-up place under some bushes and buried the papers there."

He gazed steadily at her for a long moment of silence, then wagged his head. Whatever that meant he left her to guess as he said, "You're hard as rock, Annabelle. I never knew a woman like you before."

"How many women have you known, Oliver?"

He was unprepared for that and briefly turned his back on her to study the land, then he turned back. "Not too many," he admitted. "None as tough as you are."

"I'm not tough," she told him. "I'm

desperate. If Frank Garn gets the deed and the will, Walt and I'll have absolutely nothing. We pawned everything we had just to get out here, and when we arrived we didn't have enough money left to even buy new boots. That's why we're wearing moccasins. An Indian woman sold us two pairs for half a cartwheel. You understand? If we lose our inheritance we'll be destitute. Ragged, hungry in a strange country, and destitute."

He smiled a little. "You'll never be destitute, Annabelle. You'll always manage. Whether you believe it or not, you're tough an' savvy."

She caught him unprepared again. "I doubt that you're right but I certainly hope you are. Oliver; tell me about that gun with the stag handles." As his expression changed, it was her turn to smile a little. "You didn't want to talk about it back there. Walt accepted that. He's sleeping. Women are different. They don't function according to the masculine code."

He nodded slightly. "Different," he

murmured, then, in a stronger voice he said, "Didn't your folks teach you it's bad manners to pry into other people's business an' to ask personal questions?"

"Yes," she said quietly. "They did."

"Why do you want to know?"

"Because I need to make up my mind about you."

They gazed unwaveringly at one another for a long time; meanwhile that puny pink streak miles distant along the far horizon had begun to widen, to assume a stronger shade of dawn-pink, and to firm up.

Oliver gently wagged his head. "You don't have to make a judgment about me, Annabelle. If we get out of this mess alive, you'n Walt will go your way an' I'll go mine. In years to come maybe each of us'll sit on a porch come evening somewhere, and remember, but even that'll get dim as time passes."

She listened to him with her head slightly to one side, her expression quizzical. "Would you care to know what I've thought about since you came back with those horses last night; rode along for hours thinking about?"

He hung fire. He didn't like this conversation, did not want to prolong it. Besides, daylight was nigh, they'd have to get back to practical things like keeping ahead and staying alive.

She brushed his silence aside. "If we come through this, Oliver, and if we dig up the will and the deed, get Uncle Henry's ranch back, we're going to need a seasoned cowman to ramrod things for us."

He got a vertical line between his eyes. "You'll find one, Annabelle. This part of the world's full of experienced stockmen."

"I want you, Oliver."

He knew her well enough by now to understand how powerfully opinionated she could be. "Annabelle, listen to me. You're a girl, a greenhorn in this part of the country. There's a lot you don't know and most likely wouldn't understand. I'm fond of you. I like your brother too, but you're somethin' different. If I could do it, I'd take up your offer, but I just plain can't."

She pointed out. "It's the gun, isn't it?"

"What do you mean?"

"You're an outlaw, aren't you?"

He felt cold air against his bruised cheek, felt it down inside his shirt.

"It doesn't matter, Oliver."

"Annabelle, take my word for it. It does matter."

"All right," she said resolutely. "Walt can have the ranch and I'll go with you. Out to California. Maybe back east to New York or some place where they've never heard of you."

He was shocked. "Annabelle, what in the hell are you — ?"

Her teeth flashed in a bold smile at him. "You're resourceful, clever, shrewd and blind as a damned bat, Oliver."

He stared, completely afraid to believe what instinct was telling him. She gave him no opportunity to speak.

"Why do you think I stood out under

that tree half the night until you got back with those horses?"

"Because I told you to."

She snorted. "Oliver, if you told me not to, I'd still have stood out there with my insides tied in knots for fear something would happen to you down there."

He was completely at a loss and remained that way until she suddenly raised an arm and said, "There they are."

6

Too Many Horses

SHE was half right; there were two riders coming south with the steady wind at their backs, too distant for much to be made out about them except that they rode side by side, hunched inside coats atop horses that did not like the wind either.

Oliver squatted with his back to the girl and concentrated on the horsemen. In a while they would be closer and the pre-dawn light would be better, but right now although he had an odd feeling about those two riders, they were either paralleling the Lee-Dunhill shod-horse sign or were riding a few yards east of it. At that distance it was difficult to be sure of much of anything except that they would come very close to the bosque of oaks.

Annabelle quietly left him to go back and warn her brother. When Oliver turned to speak, she was gone. He looked farther back through the shadows, then grunted and turned back to watching the horsemen.

False dawn provided adequate visibility up close. Oliver saw the pair of riders halt and sit for a while, then resume their course but angling more to their left. That, he told himself, was because they had finally found the shod-horse tracks and were now following them. But they did not ride fast and made no attempt to seek shelter, of which the only decent amount was up ahead where Oliver was squatting and watching.

Both men had booted carbines slung beneath their *rosaderos*. Both were hunched down inside sheep-pelt riders' coats, flesh side out. Both wore roping-gloves and had blanket-rolls behind their cantles.

Oliver breathed deeply with relief. Neither of those men was Frank Garn. In fact neither of them had the appearance of either Garn or his riders, and both men were riding either black or seal-brown horses.

Annabelle spoke behind him. "Who are they?"

He didn't know. "Maybe riders passing along looking for work. Maybe local stockmen heading to town. How's your brother?"

"Tired but won't admit it. Oliver? That should be a grulla and a bay. If that isn't Garn where is he?"

"Damned if I know, but if he came up out of the canyon and saw those two, sure as hell by now he'd have made a run on them or gone into hiding."

Annabelle squatted beside him. "They're following our tracks."

"Yes'm, they sure are. Maybe they'll have somethin' to eat instead of jerky." He stood up. "Go on back to your brother. Just to make damned sure I'll let them ride past an' when they see you two I'll be behind them. If they're harmless, fine. If not I'll still be behind them."

The wind seemed to diminish a little

as dawn arrived and the pair of mounted strangers turned toward the stand of oaks.

Oliver faded back, let the tie-down over his hip-holstered gun hang slack, blended among the dark-boled trees and waited.

The strangers halted a few yards out, peering in among the trees where night-gloom still lingered. They were not young men, one was thicker than the other, or seemed to be inside his sheep-pelt coat, and as Oliver watched they both did a prudent thing, they unbuttoned the lower part of their coats, folded the leather back to reveal holstered sixguns, and tugged loose their tiedowns, all things Oliver accepted as being perfectly natural under the circumstances.

They approached the trees side by side, working their way among them within sight of Annabelle and her brother, and kept their attention upon those two as they passed the place where Oliver was standing.

He allowed them to reach the Lees

81

before stepping soundlessly closer behind them. The strangers were amiable individuals. As they dismounted they eyed Walt and asked if he was feeling all right. Walt exclaimed that he was and his sister quietly contradicted him by saying, "He had a fever a few days back. He's weak but much better."

"Well now", stated one of the men, grey at the temples, craggy-faced with shrewd eyes. "My name's Clavenger. This here is Lester Moore. We might have just what your brother needs, young lady."

They tied their animals, Clavenger dug in his saddlebags, brought forth a bottle of malt whiskey and smilingly handed it to Walt. "Help yourself, friend. If it don't rejuvenate you right off it'll at least fortify you against this consarned wind."

Walt took two swallows and Clavenger was right, on an empty stomach it rejuvenated him almost immediately. Annabelle handed back the bottle as the other rider fished in a shirt pocket, withdrew a folded paper and spread it out to show to the Lees. You ever seen this gent, folks?"

Neither of the Lees spoke for a moment. Neither of them showed any expression at all as they stared at the picture of Oliver Dunhill before he'd gone without shaving. Walt finally said, "That's an awful big reward. What did he do?"

"Right there," stated Lester Moore, "it says bank robbery." He leaned to push the dodger closer to Walt's face. "Two thousand reward by the bank up in Arapahoe, Montana, where he made off with nine thousand dollars." Lester Moore carefully re-folded the dodger, pocketed it and eyed Walt and Annabelle. "We been a while trackin' him."

Clavenger held out a gloved hand palm up. There was a little steel circlet on his palm with a star in the centre of it and the letters US Marshal engraved around the circlet. Clavenger smiled.

"That nine thousand was an army payroll. The government's got an interest in catchin' him and recoverin' the money."

Walt and his sister exchanged a quick look, then he shook his head. "Nope. Never saw him. But if you gents'll sit down I'd like to tell you our story."

Oliver had been watching the amiable greying older man who did not sit down, but stood trailing the reins to his horse while gazing past the Lees where three saddle horses were dozing.

But Clavenger made no comment about two people having three saddle horses. He sat down and as Oliver faded farther back, listening to Walter Lee and his sister explain who they were and why they were hiding among the oaks in the middle of nowhere, he studied the lawman. He had never seen either of them before.

When they'd finished, Clavenger and Moore exchanged a look before Lester Moore said, "We saw the mouth of the canyon back a ways. Seemed a likely place for a man to hide, an' there were tracks goin' down there but they looked old. Or maybe the wind scoured them into lookin' that way. What we really want to find is a town with a telegraph office in it."

Both the Lees had been to the only town less than a hundred miles away, a stockmen's settlement named Paloverde, but, as they told the federal deputies, there was no telegraph office down there.

The wind was diminishing to fitful little bursts that ran close to the ground. The sun was in place, still very low on its predictable climbing curve; the pair of lawmen willingly relaxed among the oaks because they'd been in the saddle since two or three hours before sunup and at least one of them, Howard Clavenger, who could smell uneasiness in human beings from a hundred yards, after having listened to the Lees' dilemma, filled a foul little pipe from an elk-hide pouch, smoked and studied the brother and sister, and the three horses, only one of which had a full rig up-ended in the shadows, and trickled smoke, while

Oliver remained far back wondering how he could get his mule-nosed bay horse, his outfit, and get the hell away from here.

He decided he wasn't going to be able to do it as long as the deputy US marshals were unwilling to ride on. He also noticed Annabelle's uneasiness and cursed under his breath because he'd made a very accurate appraisal of the big, amiable man named Clavenger, a professional manhunter right down to the heels of his boots, who wouldn't miss something like that.

No one, including Oliver Dunhill, was prepared for what happened as the wind dwindled and the sun climbed, bringing heat into the new day. Oliver wouldn't have expected it even if the lawman hadn't arrived to divert his entire attention, but probably the most surprised people among the oaks were Howard Clavenger and Lester Moore.

Three men on foot appeared from the west, concealed by the oaks until they no longer cared about concealment and marched in among the trees with guns cocked and beard-stubbled, drawn faces set in uncompromising lines. Oliver did not see them until one of them spoke harshly in a voice faintly tainted with a Texas accent.

"That there is a nice, chummy gatherin', folks. Now you just set there with your hands in plain sight and keep quiet."

The speaker moved into plain sight of the seated people, behind Annabelle and her brother but clearly visible to the pair of federal lawmen. He eyed the strangers with a faint scowl, looked at their horses and allowed his nearly lipless mouth to form a faint smile. "In case you got some idea of gettin' rank," he told the frozen strangers, "I got a couple of friends back a ways with carbines." The man moved up behind Walt and studied the strangers. "Thought there was just one of you," he said. "Well, it don't matter. Frank'll be along directly. He rode up out of the canyon an' us three climbed out west of here just in case you hadn't got this far south yet, so's we could set up an ambush. This is even better." The rangeman returned to studying the horses. "Someone's missin'," he said. "There's five horses an' four of you folks." He frowned at the pair of lawmen. "Where's the other feller?"

Marshal Clavenger's pipe had gone out; he very slowly fished for a match, re-lit it and gazed at the man with the gun through fragrant, rising smoke. He did not mention that this same problem had been worrying him. Instead, he said, "Who is Frank?"

The gun-handy rider answered off-handedly. "Frank Garn, the head man. Him an' a feller named Andy'll be comin' down-country directly on horseback." He flicked his gun carelessly in the direction of the dozing horses. "That sorrel with the roached mane belongs to Frank. That bay horse was stolen from us last night too, by these folks and someone else. One of you gents, maybe."

Clavenger puffed and pondered, eyed the Lees and finally spoke again, "Why are you after these folks?"

The cowboy fixed Clavenger with a surly glare. "They're thieves, that's why. They stole some valuable papers from the ranch an' Frank wants 'em back."

Oliver heard a distant sound in his hiding-place of speckled shade and shadows. He craned northward and this time the pair of approaching horsemen were moving through good visibility. One of them was the lanky individual he'd left lying in the moonlight. The other one was unmistakably Frank Garn.

Others had either picked up the sound or had seen movement up yonder. The other two rangemen slipped from concealment into plain sight. One of them ignored the seated people to walk eastward among the trees until he saw the horsemen, then he returned with a gloating call. "Took 'em long enough but they're coming."

This announcement seemed to stiffen the resolve of the man with the Texas accent. He flicked his gun and gave an order. "Toss your weapons toward me. Be real careful." His companions palmed their Colts just in case but there was no threat from the lawmen nor the Lees. When they were all disarmed the three rangemen came closer. One of them walked toward the eastern edge of the bosque to await the arrival of the riders. The other two hunkered down eyeing Clavenger and Moore. "Who are you gents?" one of them asked, and before anyone could answer he also said, "There was on'y one set of tracks. You can explain that if you're of a mind to."

Neither Clavenger nor his companion knew what their interrogator was talking about, but Oliver did where he was south of the others well concealed among oak trees.

Clavenger surprised Oliver and everyone else with his answer. He had been a lawman for many years, there were almost no situations he had not been through. This one was no exception. He gave an answer that was adequate without revealing anything.

"Wasn't any call for both of us to scout around."

The Texan's answer was blunt. "Out where there ain't no law, mister, do you know what folks do to men who steal their horses in the night?"

Clavenger did not bat an eye. "You got a match, friend? My pipe went out again."

The rangeman tossed over a big wooden match and watched sulphur-smoke rise as the older man got his pipe fired up again. Clavenger was apologetic. "Darned near impossible to carry on conversation an' smoke a pipe at the same time, isn't it?"

The man with the accent did not reply; his companion did. He was a sinewy, weathered man with startlingly blue eyes in a perpetually sun-bronzed face. "You stole them horses, didn't you?"

The unruffled, sturdy lawman turned his attention to the speaker while puffing. "You're talkin' about that bay yonder an' the sorrel with the roached mane?"

"You know which horses I'm talkin'

about. Beatin' around the bush won't keep you from gettin' yanked up by the neck."

Clavenger tamped his pipe's contents with a calloused thumb. Before he could answer, if that had been his intention, a man's sharp call from beyond the bosque eastward caught everyone's attention. Both the rangemen stood up craning in the direction of the raised voices.

Oliver recognised one of those voices. It was gruff, growly and disagreeable. Frank Garn. He knelt beside an old oak to watch the men on horseback swing to the ground, palaver with the man who had walked out to meet them, then start forward among the trees.

He distinctly heard Garn say, "There wasn't no sign of two riders. Are you sure these two was with the others?"

The answer he got back was diffident. "Can't be real sure of nothin' around here, Frank, but when we snuck up over the edge of the canyon and come onto 'em in the trees, there was the girl, her brother an' them other two."

Oliver's heart did a flip-flop when Garn growled at the lanky man beside him, "You saw the one that stole the horses an' beat you. Point him out to me."

When the three men came up, Garn and his companion leading horses, not a word was said as the lanky man with the puffy lips and tired eyes looked at both Clavenger and Moore. He said, "It happened like I told you, Frank. Real fast, an' about all I seen real good was his face. He had the start of a pretty fair beard."

Neither of the lawmen was bearded. In fact both of them were not only clean-shaven, but had shaved very recently.

Garn handed his reins to one of his riders, walked among the seated people, saw empty holsters, raised his eyes to the horses and put a menacing scowl upon the pair of lawmen. "You got a friend around here somewhere?" He gestured. "One too many horses for the lot of you." He let the arm drop back to his side. "That bay and sorrel belong to us. That mule-nosed horse — who was riding him?"

Clavenger's pipe had gone out again. This time he looked for something to knock it against, and afterward as he was putting it into a pocket he looked up at Frank Garn with a totally calm expression and said, "You know as much about that mule-nosed horse as we do. All I can tell you is that me'n my friend here was ridin' south lookin' for a town when we come onto these folks. Hardly had time to more'n exchange names before your friends there came sneakin' through the trees an' caught us flat-footed." Marshal Clavenger got slowly to his feet facing Frank Garn. "We're cattle buyers from up north. We don't take kindly to bein' called horsethieves. Those animals with bedrolls behind the cantles belong to us. We got no need for your horses or anyone else's horses. I don't know what your trouble is, an' friend, I'm not interested in it. We'd like to pick up our guns an' be on our way. By the way, is there a town anywhere near?"

The big man's calm manner and forthright tone of voice impressed Garn and his riders, but their problem now had to include the 'cattle buyers'. They had two horses. Garn's riders did not need those animals now that they could recover their stolen animals, but the longer the four of them stood there considering this situation, the clearer it became that they could not allow the cattle buyers to ride away, find a town and tell folks down there what they'd encountered at Horse Canyon.

7

One Last Try

FOR Oliver, who had followed everything from hiding, Frank Garn's choices were limited. He could either let the lawmen go, believing as Oliver thought he did, that they were a pair of itinerant livestock buyers, or he could make sure they never reached a town with their story, and that meant planting them in shallow graves somewhere, probably down in Horse Canyon, alongside Annabelle and her brother.

Whether Garn would do that depended upon two things, his willingness to commit four murders, and whether he really meant to kill the Lees to get his defunct employer's will and land-deed.

Over the past few days Oliver had arrived at what he considered was a fact: Garn *would* kill the girl and her brother to protect his claim to a large cow outfit. If he would do that — what the hell — a man couldn't get hanged any higher for four killings than he could for two killings — if he got caught.

Oliver went farther back toward the southern end of the trees to roll and light a smoke while he pondered. There was another element worth considering. Garn, like the pair of federal lawmen, had found one too many horses and while the lawmen hadn't made an issue about this, Frank Garn had.

Oliver stubbed out the smoke and stood up, gazing out where sunlight was bringing early summer heat to the empty land. Until Garn was sure about that extra horse Oliver did not believe he would kill anyone.

He had to satisfy himself that there wasn't another man roaming around somewhere. If he could find him, most likely there would be a fifth grave in Horse Canyon. If he couldn't find him . . .

With the wind gone and the heat rising, thirst became a problem. Going back down into the canyon to the creek and returning would take most of what was left of the day. Unless it could be done on horseback. Oliver toyed with that idea as he slipped back within hearing distance of the camp, and got a surprise. A pair of canteens were being passed around. He hadn't noticed canteens on the rigs of the lawmen. He and the Lees had not brought canteens out of the canyon with them so he had to assume Garn and the lanky man had brought them, but their actual ownership was not very important. Their contents were. Oliver watched the canteens passing from hand to hand and had almost decided to climb back down into the canyon on foot, tank up and return when Frank Garn upended one canteen and when nothing dripped out he tossed the canteen to the man with the Texas drawl and jerked his head.

"Take 'em down to the creek an' refill 'em."

The wiry man nodded without any enthusiasm and with both canteens draped from a shoulder turned in the direction of the dozing horses.

Oliver watched the Texan mount and rein northward out of the trees. He heard the others talking, Garn's gravelly voice dominant, but hardly heeded the conversation as he considered the Texan's route back along the rim to the trail leading downward.

According to Oliver's estimate it would take the Texan more than an hour to get down to the creek. If Oliver could get due west to the rim behind the bosque of oaks without being detected, he could probably get down into the canyon long before the Texan could.

The difficulty was to cross the quarter to half a mile of open country between the bosque of oaks and the nearest rim. He figured his chances were about fifty-fifty. As long as the people in the middle of the stand of oaks were watching one another, he might be able to make it. But there were seven of them and it was expecting a lot of Providence to have all seven concentrating on one another for the half-hour or so Oliver would require to reach the rim, find a game-trail and return to the canyon's depth.

The grass was tall. He could probably belly-crawl without being detected, but belly-crawling that far would not only slow him down, it would also be very hard work. An Indian might have ignored these things and started crawling. Oliver's worry was that the time lost might result in him eventually getting down there to find that the Texan had already filled the canteens and started back.

He sat on the ground listening to the intermittent talk, alternately watching the horses and the people. The horses were hungry. They were probably also thirsty, but in either case after an hour or so of dozing in warm shade they became restless and that made Garn decide to send one of his riders out to watch them.

There was grass in the shady place but not much of it and it was pale green instead of dark green. Horses would eat it, even oak leaves, if they were hungry enough, but the man who went out to watch them tried to prevent them from moving out of a bunch and that increased their exasperation. He finally called out for help and Garn sent his remaining rider out there.

Oliver watched the situation change where the lawmen, the Lees and Frank Garn were sitting. He balanced his chance of sneaking up behind Garn. If he could do this the others might detect him but there was little possibility of them saying anything. They had reason to want Frank Garn immobilised even more than Oliver did.

The joker in this situation was that Garn's horse-tenders were in view of the others. Unless Oliver could immobilise Garn silently, without attracting the attention of his riders, he would very likely get himself shot.

But he arose, dusted his britches and began circling around to the west, far enough out through the trees to be invisible. His decision had been prompted more by exasperation than prudence, but under the circumstances, with Garn's men dispersed, it would probably be the only chance he'd have before the man returned with the canteens and before the horse-watchers got their animals sufficiently settled to permit them to return to camp.

As Annabelle had said, Dunhill was not a gambling man unless the stakes involved something more than greenbacks or silver.

In his calculations Oliver had overlooked the natural inhabitants of the oak grove. He was far enough westerly to begin his approach when some nesting birds, made uneasy by his silent stalking, rose into the air squawking loudly.

Oliver went to ground, gun in hand, watching dead ahead where anyone coming to investigate would appear. Providence, or perhaps some natural force which governed such things as bird-nests with eggs in them, sent along several large, black crow-like big birds to hover in the vicinity of the unguarded nests and their arrival aroused an even more violent reaction among the nesting birds.

Oliver saw a man with a Winchester moving among the trees, ignored the overhead diving, squawking and wheeling birds to watch. It was not Garn so it had to be one of the horse-tenders.

Evidently drawn by the noisy birds the man stopped about a hundred feet from where Oliver was lying with his cocked Colt aimed belt-buckle high, looked upwards through the leafy canopy, watched for a long time, then spat, slung the Winchester in the bend of an arm and went trudging back, satisfied the birds had not been signalling the whereabouts of an alien creature, but were fighting among themselves.

Oliver let his head drop briefly into the grass before leathering the handsome gun, getting back to his feet and watching the back of the withdrawing scout.

He began his eastward stalk, taking plenty of time to make sure he remained screened by trees and made no noise. He saw Annabelle first. She was sitting with her back against an oak with her brother nearby. Neither of them spoke nor took their eyes off the men a short distance in front of them.

Walt looked tired. For that matter so did his sister. She had dark circles under her eyes. Oliver shook his head to himself. She would be dragged behind wild horses before she'd ever admit she was exhausted. The toughness, willingness and indomitable will he had admired in her, was more courage of the spirit than physical strength.

He was learning more about the girl as time passed, but his biggest lesson was yet to come, and when it did he'd be too astonished to speak.

Frank Garn's harsh voice sounded over the report of his scout. "Birds maybe," he said. "But he's around somewhere, an' if he wasn't one of these stock buyers then he's sure as hell that feller who stole our horses and larruped hell out of Andy."

For a while there was silence. Oliver saw Garn moving among the trees, unkempt, unshaven, venomous and deadly, right up to the moment when he halted in front of Annabelle and her brother to stand glaring for a moment before addressing them. Until now he'd had other things on his mind, such as the two stalwart captives, the need for water, anxiety, and probably fear too because someone was unaccounted for. But now he had time to pursue the objective which had kept him on the trail so long.

He looked longest at the girl. "Now we're goin' to end this," he told her. "Give me those papers."

No one asked what papers he was talking about because not even the alleged livestock buyers were ignorant of what Garn meant. His two riders were standing a short distance away watching the pair of lawmen who, in turn, were alternatively watching their guards and Frank Garn.

"I'm not goin' to ask you again," Garn snarled at the girl. "You hand 'em over or I'll strip you bare in front of everyone until I find them."

Annabelle met the fierce glare without flinching or speaking, but her brother had no illusions about Frank Garn. He said, "She don't have them."

Garn turned on him. "You got 'em! All right; you dig them out or I'm goin' to blow your head off." Garn accompanied this statement with the act of drawing his sixgun.

Walt was white. So was his sister. She finally addressed Garn. "He doesn't have them either."

"Where are they?"

"Buried under some rocks."

"Where?"

"Down in the canyon in a thicket where we camped when Walt got sick with a fever."

Garn bored the girl with an unwavering stare. "You're lying. You got 'em on you."

She flared up at him. "No! I told you the truth. When Walt got sick and couldn't be moved we knew you'd catch up so we dug a hole, lined it with rock and buried the will and the deed."

Out where Oliver was lying, the ring of truth was unmistakable. But he was watching Frank Garn, thumb-pad resting atop the hammer of his gun. If Garn reached for the girl he meant to kill him.

But Garn did not move. He stared at the girl, who stared back, and finally the big man with the cold pipe between his teeth broke the stand-off. "She's telling you the truth."

Garn snarled at the big man. "How do you know?"

"Because I've spent most of my life learning when folks are lyin' and when they're not."

Oliver saw Garn's tree-shadowed face loosen slightly. He glared at Walt. "If she's lyin' you know what's goin' to happen to her, don't you?"

Walt nodded. "She told you the truth. If you shoot us now you'll never find the hole where we buried those papers."

The big man spoke again. "Mister

Garn, we don't much want to go down into the canyon with you, but if you're goin' to dig up those papers you better take us with you because if you don't an' we can find a town, we're goin' to come back with the law an' a posse."

The bruised, tired-looking lanky man Oliver had worked over, spat amber and twisted toward Garn. "One last try," he said. "We come a hell of a distance an' put up with a lot, an' now you got 'em. Let's make one last try an' if she lied to you, I'm leavin' an' you can do whatever you want to do."

The other rangeman nodded his head in agreement with the tall man but did not express himself. It was the big, greying lawman who finally said, "End of trail, Mister Garn."

Oliver watched Frank Garn turn on the big man with bared teeth. "You keep buttin' in an' you're goin' to spend eternity right here."

But Garn's threat did not come across to Oliver as menacing as some of the other things he had said.

Annabelle spoke again. "You can have the will and the deed. You can have my uncle's ranch. My brother is sick and I'm tired to the bone."

Garn walked back where his riders were sitting and stood in scowling thought. The big lawman got his pipe fired up again and concentrated on keeping it burning this time as he and his companion watched Garn. They could see his face but Oliver could not. He was behind them and Garn's back was to him when Garn finally made his decision and snarled an order to his riders. "Bring in the horses. We're goin' back down there. Like you said, Andy, this is our last attempt." He jutted a square jaw in the direction of the lawmen. "You ride in front where we can keep an eye on you." He turned, looked out among the trees and swore under his breath. He was still worried about that mule-nosed bay horse whose rider was not accounted for.

8

An Interruption

OLIVER watched them ride away from the oaks in a northward direction and got the distinct impression that Frank Garn was pleased to be leaving. He was still worrying about the owner of the bay horse he was leading by the reins.

Oliver wagged his head. If Garn hadn't been over his head in difficulties he would have rummaged through the saddlebags on the bay horse.

If their position had been reversed that would have been the first thing Oliver would have done. It would have established the identity of the horse's owner whether Garn ever found him or not, and as Oliver turned back in the direction of the canyon's rim he had wanted to approach before but dared not, for the first time since the oak grove had filled up with people he felt that there was an excellent chance that he could set up an ambush down there near the creek.

His search for a game-trail down from the plateau consumed quite a bit of time. The barranca was particularly steep this far south, but eventually he located an old trail which he thought had probably been made by Indians many years earlier and had not been used much by animals since. It was steep. It also gave Oliver an excellent overview of the canyon's width. He was looking for the man Garn had sent to fill the canteens but did not find him.

He could still be down there, undergrowth was particularly dense where Oliver was descending, although it seemed unlikely he would have come this far down the creek to fill the canteens.

Most important to Oliver was the fact that the man should not see him coming down the old trail backgrounded by a tan-tawny cliff-face, a perfect target.

He was not shot at, nor did he see any movement below as he paused once on the downward climb to rest beside a precariously balanced big rock. Here, he heard the familiar rattle that let him know he had trespassed, and stepped away from the rock without ever locating the snake.

Thirst was heightened by the position of the sun against the cliff face behind him. He picked up the gait a little after he felt confident no one had seen him or, if they had, were more interested in their own concerns than his.

There was no reason for haste, except for thirst. Garn would have to ride north to that more distant trail, descend it, then work his way southward another couple of miles. This was one of those instances when a man on foot could make better time then men on horseback.

By the time he reached the bottom of the wide canyon the sun was already slanting off centre. It had been pleasant in among the oaks. It hadn't been unbearably hot away from them atop the plateau, but down in the canyon the heat was solid.

Oliver cared for first things first. He dropped belly-down at creekside and drank, reared back to listen and look around, then ducked his head to drink again. There was no substitute for water, especially when a man had been without it a long time on a hot summer day.

He remained prone against soft, moist earth for a few minutes before arising and moving clear of the trees, willows and brush to orient himself. He was south of the big thicket where he'd first encountered Walt Lee.

That was in his favour. The men who were by now down in the canyon coming southward, would be north of him. He liked the idea of them being in front, attributed this to a kindly fate who had finally decided to lend Oliver a hand, and got a rude shock when the underbush west of him shook and rattled as some large creature forced its way through toward the opposite side of the creek.

He hoped very hard it would not be some belligerent creature like a bear because although he could shoot it in self-protection the echo of a gunshot down here would carry easily up where Garn and his companions were riding. All he'd need to reveal his presence and scotch a successful dry gulch would be one gunshot.

He moved farther back, watched the place where the creature was pitching its weight against wiry underbrush and finally drew his sixgun. If it was a bear it was a noisy one; probably a boar bear. They feared nothing, rarely tried to conceal their presence and would fight a buzz-saw.

Oliver felt wiry underbrush behind him, turned very fleetingly to see whether or not it would provide him with cover, decided it would and twisted, pushed, leaned his way past the initial growth and stood in the heart of the thicket with just his head showing.

The big animal yonder across the creek was breaking clear. Oliver aimed high and waited. It was not a bear, it was a horse, one with a saddle on its back. At first it seemed that the horse was riderless, but as it finally broke clear and lunged toward water, Oliver saw the wiry man holding to its tail. It was the man with the slight accent who had been sent to the creek for water.

Oliver lowered his weapon, holstered it and scowled. The Texan or whatever he was, was a long mile farther down the creek than he'd had to go just to fill canteens.

He didn't fill the canteens. He left them looped around the saddlehorn, got upstream of his thirsty, sweaty horse, tossed his hat aside and got belly-down.

Oliver let him swallow several times before giving a warning without raising his voice. "Just stay down like that, cowboy. Keep your hands up ahead and finish drinking."

The wiry man raised his head off the ground like a lizard and twisted to look across the creek where Oliver was gingerly extricating himself from

115

his protective thicket. He did not do as Oliver had said, finish drinking, because he was no longer thirsty.

When they were facing each other across the creek Oliver gestured with his handgun. "Toss your Colt away. Fine, now stand up."

As the cowboy arose to his full height, which was somewhat less than Oliver's height, his eyes widened. "Hell, you'll be that feller — "

"I sure will, an' your friends are comin' south down along the creek, should be showin' up within the next hour or two."

The Texan seemed not to have heard as he stared at Oliver. "You stole our horses. You larruped Andy. That mule-nosed horse up in the oaks belonged to you."

"You're doin' pretty good," Oliver replied with a smile.

"What'n hell are they comin' down this far for?"

Oliver continued to smile when he replied, "Why'd you come this far south just to fill the canteens?"

The wiry, older man closed his mouth like a bear-trap.

Oliver said, "Lead your horse across to this side of the creek, and if you get clever I'll bust your head like a pumpkin."

Evidently Oliver's powerful build, even without the gun in his fist, impressed the cowboy because he waded the creek leading his horse and stopped to bat at mosquitoes his crossing had aroused.

He had recovered from his astonishment. He was a resourceful, craggy, weathered man with shrewd eyes and a wide mouth surrounded by leathery skin. When Oliver repeated the question about the man being much farther southward then he'd had to go, the cowboy's habitually squinted eyes got nearly closed as he regarded his captor. He said nothing.

Oliver considered the rangeman. Before he could decide on a course of action the cowboy said, "You give Andy a hell of a shellacking."

"I wouldn't have had to if the damned

fool hadn't thought he could jump a man with a gun in his fist." Oliver cocked his head slightly to one side, making a judgment about the cowboy. "How about you?" Oliver held both arms away from his sides. "Here's your chance."

But the wiry man grinned as he wagged his head. "No thanks. Andy's one hell of a brawler. If you whipped him . . ."

Oliver continued to study the shorter, older man for a moment or two before addressing him again. "You still haven't answered my question, an' friend, time's gettin' short." He folded his hands together and loudly cracked his knuckles while staring at the shorter man.

The cowboy was rooted in place. Oliver shrugged and started forward. The cowboy had an immediate change of heart. "If I had my weapon it'd be different," he said, but without much conviction as Oliver stopped in front of him. "Go over there an' get it," he told the rangerider. "Go ahead."

"If Frank's comin' you don't want no gunshots wakin' up the countryside, mister."

Oliver smiled thinly. "Go — get — it!"

"So's you can pot-shot me in the back as I'm crossin' the creek?"

"Nope. I'll give you an even chance."

The cowboy's gaze dropped to the gun with the bluing still on it and the expensive grips, raised his eyes and gently wagged his head. He gestured with his left arm up the creek. "Them folks had a camp in the brush up yonder. I was figurin' on studyin' it. For seven years I was a sign-reader an' tracker for the army."

"What did you find?" Oliver asked.

"Nothing. My horse commenced actin' silly so I led him south lookin' for a break in the willows and underbrush so's he could drink because I figured he was thirsty again." The cowboy's leathery face split into a death's-head grin. "An' there you was, so I guess it wasn't thirst that got him upset, it was your scent."

"Well now, that's not very complimentary, is it? How much scuffin' around did you do at the camp?"

The man's shrewd eyes were fixed on Oliver's face through an interval of silence, then he said, "By gawd, there *is* somethin' up there, ain't there? They left somethin' behind like I figured on the ride down here they might have." The man's probing squint remained fixed on Oliver's face. "Them damned papers. How'd *you* know?"

"Heard the girl tell Garn they were down here."

"Ah . . . You *are* the feller who owned that mule-nosed bay horse. You was hidin' among the trees up yonder."

Oliver loosened a little. He had felt dispassionate interest in the rangeman from the beginning, but now he was also beginning to feel a little respect for the man's shrewdness. He'd figured something out Frank Garn hadn't even believed when Annabelle had told him: where the will and deed were buried.

Oliver produced the makings, rolled

a smoke and offered the sack to the cowboy, but the older man shook his head and fished forth a lint-encrusted plug of molasses-cured, worried off a little and tongued it up into his cheek, spat once, replaced the plug and smiled at Oliver. They had been talking for about fifteen minutes, enough time for whatever fear the cowboy may have initially felt, to have atrophied. He made a suggestion to Oliver. "If we got enough time I think I can find that hidin' place. I done things like that for seven years, mister. Sniffed out caches of weapons, read brushed-over places where broncos cached food."

Oliver perceptibly inclined his head. "Lead the way, an' just for the hell of it leave your gun in the mud over there."

The older man was agreeable. "No sense to buckin' our way back through that damned underbrush, we can go up this side of the creek." As he started ahead leading the horse the man also said, "You know that girl an' her brother?"

"I know them."

"Well, supposin' we find their cache and get old Henry's will an' that deed to his land?"

"Supposin' you just keep walkin'."

Oliver eyed the position of the sun, made some rough calculations and thought they might have about an hour before the sound of Frank Garn and his companions would be audible.

He could have anticipated a lot of things happening down in Horse Canyon, but what he was doing now would not have been one of them. As he eyed the wiry man he said, "What's your name?"

"Charley Hunter."

"That's a good name for someone who hunts folks down."

"Yeah. I thought so when I started using it. What's your name?"

"Oliver."

"Oliver what?"

They had reached the big thicket and had a path into it in sight when Oliver said, "Tie the horse."

The older man obeyed then pushed ahead into the centre of the thicket where Oliver had first met Annabelle's brother. He stopped and turned his head slowly from side to side like a bird-dog. Oliver was beginning to worry about the oncoming riders and said, "They dug out a place in the ground, lined it with rocks and buried the papers there, then covered it up."

Charley Hunter continued to scan the area from narrowed eyes until he saw several places where flat stones had been moved from their age-old bed, then he smiled. "I think we got it, Mister Oliver." He went over, pushed aside some wiry limbs of underbrush and pointed to the outlines in the soil where stones had been moved.

He got down on his knees and began stirring the earth. When he found a place where the soil was not compacted he reared back on his haunches and grinned upwards, then leaned forward and clawed like a badger, uncovered a flat stone the size of a dinner-plate, swept soft dirt away from it, lifted it out and leaned forward. Oliver had to step to one side in order to be able to see around the older man.

Charley Hunter gloated as he lifted out some papers that were wrinkled and limp. "We been damned near a full month tryin' to catch those whelps an' get these here things." He handed them up to Oliver then levered himself upright and leaned to study what he had uncovered. Oliver thought he was reading them until he said, "What do they say?"

People who could not read were common even in towns, but among frontiersmen of any kind who'd spent most of their lives living out of saddlebags, the rarity was not to find someone who could not read, the rarity was to come across someone who could.

Oliver read the will aloud. Charley Hunter did not move nor make a sound. But when Oliver began reading the land-deed the cowboy screwed up his face and looked at Oliver. "What'n hell does all them numbers mean?"

Oliver was folding the papers to pocket

them when he replied. "Survey figures. Metes and bounds. They tell how far a man can go in one straight line before he has to make a turn an' go in another straight line."

Charley continued to look totally perplexed. "Why didn't they just sashay around a tree or a big rock an' bend around so's it'd make sense."

"Because surveys are made in straight lines. They don't bend around."

"That's silly, ain't it?"

Oliver looked at the rangeman. "Yeah, I guess so."

Charley demonstrated another attribute. He held up a calloused hand. "Riders coming."

He had excellent hearing.

9

Face-Down!

MOMENTS after Charley mentioned hearing approaching riders Oliver also heard them. He told the cowboy to cover the hole and as this was being done he stepped aside for a better view of the upper country. Charley spoke from a kneeling position where he'd made the cache look as though it hadn't been raided. He had his own interests to consider.

"Mister Oliver, now that you got them papers what d'you figure to do with 'em?"

Oliver was trying to see movement through the underbrush and tree-shadows northward when he replied. "Give 'em to the Lees."

Charley seemed to have expected that reply. He said, "What'll *they* do with 'em? Frank Garn's still goin' to kill to get 'em."

Oliver finally saw riders. They were strung out with the pair of lawmen up front and Garn far enough back to keep an eye on everyone else. He looked over where the cowboy had finished masking the raided cache and said, "Well, I guess if they can find a county seat and get the papers recorded, Garn will have lost out and — "

"That's not goin' to keep him from killin' 'em," the cowboy said. "You don't know Frank. He don't give up an' he figures to own the outfit come hell or high water. Mister Oliver, how did you get caught up with them folks?"

Oliver was watching the distant horsemen passing in and out of sunshine and shade. He faced the rangeman briefly as he said, "Met 'em in this canyon." He did not mention the reason he'd met the Lees was because Annabelle Lee had tried to steal his horse.

The rangeman shrugged. "That ain't much of an attachment, is it?"

"Meanin' what?"

"Meanin', why maybe get yourself killed for folks you don't hardly know? You don't owe them anything."

Oliver was turning away from the cowboy as he answered in a dry tone of voice. "No, I don't owe 'em anything, except maybe a little help when a son of a bitch is out to kill 'em both an' steal their inheritance."

Charley Hunter let the subject die. He stood concealed from view of the oncoming riders by the thicket, which in most places was taller than he was.

Oliver decided his tracks would be noticed as soon as Garn and his remaining two riders broke through the thicket where the campsite was. He jerked his head for the rangeman to precede him back the way they had come, and when they were beside the cowboy's horse Oliver pondered the fate of his unwanted companion.

Charley, probably suspecting something, wagged his head. "As far as me'n the other boys is concerned, Frank's about wore us out tryin' to get them damned papers. I think if you called Frank the other boys wouldn't take up for him."

Oliver considered Charley Hunter wryly. "If I had nine lives I might take a chance on that." He turned and watched the riders halt beyond the thicket where Annabelle and her brother dismounted to lead the way. Offhandedly he said, "Charley, did you know those two big fellers aren't livestock buyers?"

"They aren't?"

"They're deputy US marshals."

Charley snapped straight up to his full height. "No! How'n hell could that be?"

"They're on a trail," Oliver replied. "I saw that big older feller's badge before you'n your friends got down to the oaks."

"You're makin' this up."

"No, it's the gospel truth."

The wiry, older man could hear voices up where the new arrivals were threading their way into the clearing. Oliver's revelation had upset him badly. He and

Oliver listened for a while then Oliver nudged the cowboy and started walking toward the eastward barranca. That was the only place he could achieve sufficient elevation to see what was happening at the campsite. It was also the best place to establish his ambush.

Charley trudged along looking worried. He had nothing more to say until they were climbing a game-trail, and stopped when they reached a rocky place with a stunted old tree offering meagre shade.

As they moved into speckled shade Oliver saw someone quartering before striking out over the fresh sign of two men wearing boots. He told Charley that tracker was going to find his tethered horse.

That made the wiry rangeman flinch. For a moment or two he was quiet as he watched the people in the clearing. Annabelle's brother scuffed around, ignoring the others, until he came to the place where he'd made his cache, then he dropped down with Frank Garn and the pair of captured lawmen watching, and did as Charley Hunter had done, began to dig like a badger. When he discovered the topmost stone he looked up and said something. Garn placed his sixgun against Walt's neck and snarled. Walt leaned to lift out the rock.

At this moment the rider who'd back-tracked returned to the clearing with an announcement that diverted everyone. "Frank! Charley's horse is tied out yonder!"

Garn was still holding the gun when he said, "Any sign of him?"

The slightly breathless, and probably badly confused, rider shook his head. "No, but there's tracks headin' east. Two sets of tracks."

Everyone's interest was diverted, otherwise they would have noticed the look on Walt Lee's face after he'd lifted the cap-rock. He seemed to have turned to stone.

Garn said, "Two sets? Are you sure?"

The cowboy was sure. "Come see for yourself Frank . . . I don't like this."

Garn twisted slowly from the waist,

looking out and around, letting the gun hang at his side.

The lanky rider with the bruised face let go a rattling breath, did not do as the others were doing, peer in several directions. He flatly said, "Ambush, Frank."

The pair of federal lawmen were warily peering past as much of the thicket as they could see. The older one made a statement while rolling his eyes toward the east. "You rode right into it, Mister Garn."

For a long moment no one moved nor spoke. Oliver told his companion to sit on the ground in front of him, not to make a sound, and keep down. Charley watched his captor draw that fancy-handled sixgun, turned to squint in the direction of the camp and shook his head. "Too far." he told Oliver. "You should've stayed in the brush and throwed down on 'em up close."

Oliver did not reply as he stepped up beside the tree, took a rest over the wrist of his free hand which was pressed hard against the tree, and fired.

Someone down there yelled as everyone hurtled to get clear of the exposed opening. Everyone except Walt, he was still on his knees by the raided cache. Annabelle called frantically for him to dive for cover.

Oliver held his firing-stance. Charley Hunter, on the ground in front of him, fascinated by the abrupt wild activity that shot had caused, acted like he wanted to laugh until Oliver said, "You think I missed?"

"You sure did. Missed Frank by a yard. Still, that's fair shootin' for the distance."

"If I'd wanted to hit Garn I would have," Oliver replied, then raised his voice enough for it to carry to the thicket. "Garn! You're not goin' out of there if we got to keep watch on you for a month."

There was no immediate response, but eventually a growly voice called back from concealment. "Charley, is that you? What the hell do you think you're doing?"

Oliver nudged the seated man with his sixgun. "Tell him to look in the cache."

Hunter did not even hesitate before calling back. After that Garn's voice sounded again, but not very loud as he ordered Walt Lee to go over and tell him what was in the hole. Walt didn't have to expose himself. He answered Garn curtly. "It's empty. There's nothin' in it."

That announcement caused an even longer period of silence. Finally, Frank Garn swore fiercely as he yelled back to Charley Hunter that if he thought he could steal those papers and claim the land, he'd better think again about it because if he persisted Frank would track him to the ends of the earth and kill him.

Hunter didn't look happy as he twisted to squint at Oliver. The larger, younger man smiled coldly.

Garn called again. "Who's with you, Charley?"

Oliver nudged his prisoner again with his gunbarrel. "Tell him it's three bounty hunters who been campin' down in here."

"He won't believe that. They already know besides my tracks there was only one other set."

"Tell him!"

Hunter called back what he'd been told to say, and there was another long silence during which Oliver blocked in small areas of the thicket for a target. He didn't find one before Frank Garn broke into a fierce tirade against Hunter, accusing him of being a traitor and much worse. Garn was clearly in a murderous rage.

Oliver placed the approximate area of the thicket where that furious voice might be coming from, took another rest against the tree, and fired.

Charley jumped. He'd been concentrating on the tirade, had no idea Oliver was going to fire again. Afterwards he scuttled behind the tree.

It was a wise manoeuvre because this time gunfire raked the slightly higher place where Oliver's gunsmoke, soiled and faintly moving, showed where the shot had come from.

As Oliver squatted behind some rocks noting where the firing was coming from, he plugged out two spent casings and plugged in two fresh loads. Charley's face was twisted and sweat-shiny as he peered in the direction of Oliver's rocks. When the gun-thunder stopped Charley made a shrill announcement. "What you don't know about settin' up an ambush would fill one hell of a big book. They got us pinned against this damned cliff."

Oliver had reloaded and was looking for a rock-rest. He ignored the rangemen until he found one and eased up to fire off another round. "It's the other way round, Charley. We got them pinned in that thicket."

"They got horses for Cris'sake!"

"Yeah. That's what I'm waitin' for; someone to get atop a horse."

Charley subsided.

The still air smelled powerfully of burnt gunpowder. The heat was still heavily solid even though the sun had settled even lower to the rims in the west.

Frank Garn called out again. "Charley, you can ride out of here free if you'll leave them papers in plain sight."

Oliver eyed the sweating older man. "There's your chance," he said sarcastically, and Hunter blared at him. "You're goin' to get us both killed!"

Oliver replied to Garn. "You can have the papers, mister. All you got to do to get 'em is send someone down along the creek where one of us'll meet him an' with all the money you got, and your horses. You better have a lot of money, mister."

Charley looked strained. "He don't have a lot of money. What're you tryin' to do?"

"Get another prisoner. If I can get two more, that'll leave Garn by himself, an' with night comin' on, if one of those lawmen can't divert him long enough for the other one to lift his hair, I'll be real disappointed in deputy marshals."

Charley Hunter turned back toward

the camp. It still appeared empty. He sighed and groped around for his plug of chewing-tobacco.

Garn responded to Oliver's offer. "We'll get you boys after dark. Unless you got a better idea'n the one you just said."

Oliver's response was almost a drawl. "Partner, you listen real good. Countin' Charley, who's with us now, we got enough men to keep you holed up in that damned thicket until your tongue gets big as a saddle-blanket. Tonight we're comin' down there between you'n the creek. All we got to do is wait. That's your second choice. If I was in your boots I'd take the first one — all your money an' your horses."

Garn did not respond. Oliver waited, but time passed and no reply came from the thicket. He raised his head a little to look down there, but it was Charley who saw the underbrush quivering where someone was crawling northward. He pointed this out without saying a word.

Oliver saw the movement, guessed

that someone, probably Frank Garn, was trying to get out of handgun range. Or maybe get up where they'd left their horses. Either way he would gain a slight edge. If he could get away on a horse it wouldn't help him a hell of a lot. It would make him mobile but his single-tracked obsession about the legal papers would keep him trying to get them, and as far as Oliver could see, a horse would be a nuisance. It would make a target out of the man on its back.

Charley was rigidly pointing when he said "Throw one a yard in front or he's goin' to get out of there."

Oliver did not heed this advice as he squatted among the rocks watching underbrush shake as someone beneath it continued to crawl.

"You think he's goin' out of here, Charley? I don't. I think he's goin' to try an' work his way in our direction, leaving his two men to keep watch over the others . . . Tell me something, Charley; you know Garn. How good a gunhand is he?"

The older man's reply was cryptic. "Good, enough. I'll tell you somethin' about Frank Garn: once his mind's made up you can't change it with a stick of dynamite."

"Yeah. I figured that . . . Charley, do you want to go into the clearing?"

The wizened rangeman screwed up his face at Oliver. "What kind of a damn foolishness is that? They think I've throwed in with you. I wouldn't even get time to say 'howdy'."

"All right, Charley, then you better get comfortable and stay here."

"Where you goin'?"

"To meet Garn. He's not the only one who can sneak and skulk around." As Oliver said this he re-set his hat and leathered his sixgun. Charley looked uncertain so Oliver grinned at him. "Just keep out of sight. I'll be back when I can."

"*If* you can. This whole blessed thing is a mess and you're not fixin' to make it any better."

Oliver had a different idea. "Those two

men with Garn, are they as fed up with all this as you are?"

"Yes they are. Us three is rangemen an' that's all we are."

"I sure hope you're tellin' the truth, because I figure if I can take Garn out, you'n those other two won't have any fight left in you. It's a gamble, Charley, but I'm goin' to take it."

Charley snorted. "Gamble! Even if you was wrong about me — my gun's over yonder in the mud. It ain't no gamble. But you better be a real good stalker. Frank's a lot of mean things but he sure as hell ain't no greenhorn."

10

The Unexpected

THE light was deceptive this time of day even in flat country. In a steep-walled wide canyon it had a variety of deceptions such as heavy shadows on the west side of brush and timber as well as directly downward from above.

Where shadows were firming up on the west side of the farthest barranca, it was becoming more shadowy and obscure by the minute. On the east side where Oliver used every advantage to get back down off the high trail, there were patches of dusty sunlight, which he could avoid, and scraggly thickets which he utilised.

He could no longer see the brush where someone had been sneaking along. If he could have it would have provided him with a great relief. He *thought* Garn would turn easterly, but if he guessed wrong and Garn continued northward, then there probably would be no meeting.

He continued along the base of the cliff-face in fits and starts, waiting, listening and hoping. From here on he would have no advantage because he could no longer see the brush shake as someone crawled through it. He had to make a blind stalk, which was not the safest kind. But he was convinced that what he'd told Charley Hunter was true: Frank Garn's obsession with old Henry Lee's will and his land-deed would keep Garn from trying to leave the canyon on horseback without them.

If he misjudged the man, then he was going to be sneaking around down here all night for nothing. He did not expect any reassurance, but he got it when he'd gone just far enough northward to be parallel with the Lees' old camp in the thicket. Into the total stillness of Horse Canyon at this dying time of day a man's voice carried easily even though the man

143

spoke in a normal tone.

"Mister Lee, if someone raided your cache, would it have been that cowboy named Hunter?"

Walt's reply was distinct in the stillness even though neither he nor the man who'd asked the question were visible. "I been thinkin' about that. I don't know. I don't know Hunter real well. If there are other men down in here . . . But I can't imagine findin' the cache."

A third voice spoke from hiding; it was a rather whining, disgruntled voice. "You don't know Charley Hunter for a fact. Frank's a good tracker an' sign-reader but Charley used to do them things for the army. He can out-In'ian the best In'ian you ever saw. If Charley's down here, if he's lookin' for that cache, take my word for it, he found it."

After an interval of silence another voice deeper and quieter, asked a question. "Why the hell, if he got the papers, did he leave his horse tied down the creek?"

"Because we come up onto him too fast. He didn't have a chance to — "

"Naw," growled the disgruntled man. "Somethin else you don't know about Charley: he can hear a twig snap at fifty yards. We couldn't have rode up on him."

"Then why did he abandon the horse?"

"Hell I don't know. Unless that second set of tracks belonged to the same rider we couldn't find up in the clump of oaks, and that feller caught Charley and herded him away at gunpoint."

"Where was the other two? That feller said there was three of 'em down in here."

The man with the disgruntled voice answered that tartly. "You want to know? Stick your head up where they can see it."

That ended the conversation among men who could not see each other, or Oliver, who was moving again before the last remark had been made.

Daylight would linger. In fact in late springtime, early summertime, it would remain for an hour or two longer than it had only a month earlier. But that applied mostly to open country, grassed-over flat land, not a canyon.

In Horse Canyon it would linger not as direct light but as reflected light, which was uncertain at its best.

Oliver stopped advancing after he'd been at it long enough to be able to look back and orient himself by the stunted tree and the old rocks where he'd left Charley Hunter. Slanting sunlight did not reach down the easterly barranca quite that far, but the rocks, tree and the old trail they were part of were clear enough.

If Garn had turned east by now there was no way for Oliver to know it. He found a soft-limbed thicket, worked himself into concealment there, and waited. Before continuing he had to hear or see movement; otherwise, if Garn was out there also waiting, Oliver risked moving directly into his gunsight.

He was sweating. He was also tight-wound and alert. Only two things filled his mind; forcing a rendezvous and staying alive.

Somewhere in the southwesterly distance, back in the vicinity of the brush-camp, a horse lustily blew its nose. The sound carried but when the silence closed down again nothing broke it until Oliver heard several excited birds up ahead on his left. A fair distance on his left.

He blew out a long breath, mopped sweat, flicked a hungry tick off his wrist and fixed the location of those upset birds in his mind, then waited.

This time of late day birds sought roosts for the night. They did not readily leave those roosts and when they did, it was not uncommon for them to fly in a tight circle then settle back on the same branches. Birds were afraid to be caught out by darkness.

Oliver waited; the shadows moved lower in the canyon like smoke-shaded fog, not as dense but just as gloomy. More so in fact.

No more birds arose in protest as something passed through their territory.

Oliver wearied of waiting, eased out of

his thicket very carefully, got belly-down trying to ground-sluice the small height between the ground and the first shoots of the underbrush where visibility was adequate to detect movement. He smiled bleakly to himself; an Indian would have been proud of him.

He was still reluctant to move despite his urge to force things. As he'd said to Charley Hunter, he didn't have nine lives.

The waiting was bad, but somewhere around here another man was doing it, so whoever made the next move as they jockeyed for the killing advantage was likely to end up under a pile of rocks.

Oliver guessed what the cowman was doing: waiting. Lying out there somewhere like a lizard, keeping a sharp watch and waiting.

Their meeting might very well depend on whose patience gave out first.

Oliver could see beneath the brush for a fair distance even though there were spindly shadows working downward through the thickets from above. He saw a fat timber-rattler moving sluggishly toward a pile of melon-sized rocks. It offered the only alternative to nothing so he watched it. First, the snake poked its blunt snout among the lower rocks, evidently without finding what its dim brain told it was somewhere around there, then it pulled back and tried three other places before it suddenly whipped straight ahead and disappeared. Snake dens were commonly among rocks. During the time when they were shedding their skins a man could smell a den from a fair distance. Because rattlers often denned in groups, it was unwise to assume because a man saw one disappear into a jumble of rocks it would be the only one in there.

Oliver sighed. He'd seen more damned rattlesnakes in Horse Canyon than he'd ever seen in any one place before. Too bad there weren't Indians in here. They had the best way of ridding an area of rattlers. They dragged in greasewood, shoved some into any crevice they thought might have snakes, and set it afire.

More often than not those fires burned out of control over hundreds of acres, but when they stopped a man could walk just about anywhere he wanted to. If he saw snakes they were cooked.

Out of nowhere a large wood-rat, half as large as a domestic cat, came scurrying in what seemed like pure panic. Oliver watched it, turned slightly to look back in the direction it had come from, and settled his chin on the back of his hands.

Wood-rats, large though they were, were timid, illusive, not very warlike, so whatever had startled this one could have been just about anything. Oliver thought it was a man. No one's patience lasted forever.

He felt better about lying there so long as he reached back, palmed his sixgun, eased it forward and waited.

But no man-shadow appeared.

Something else did though. A fist-sized rock broke through the underbrush about two yards behind Oliver. He looked around, but very briefly. That was a schoolboy trick, but it confirmed one thing for Oliver — Garn was out there to the west and probably fairly close. A man couldn't hurl that big a stone any great distance.

If he'd thought about it Oliver would have realised he was thirsty, but instinct, or something anyway, warned him that the showdown was imminent. He was geared to that and nothing else.

In any kind of a duel some knowledge of an adversary was valuable. Oliver's opinion of the man he was trying to ambush covered several areas, but the foremost one was that Frank Garn was one of those hard-driving, remorseless men of temper and — he hoped — limited patience, because what they were both doing now had evolved into a game of out-waiting each other.

How Garn knew — or suspected — someone was out here, Oliver had no idea, except that he'd told Garn when nightfall arrived there would be movement against him.

If Garn believed there were indeed

three or four men opposing him, then it made sense that he'd tried that rock-ruse to uncover at least one of them even though no one Oliver knew would have been fooled by that schoolboy trick.

He was turning his head to the right when something snagged his vision to the left. He looked quickly in that direction and although visibility had deteriorated considerably over the last hour or so, he saw what he had been hoping to see. Someone's faint shadow moving well in advance of a four-legged creature, except that this four-legged varmint was wearing a hat.

Oliver put his own hat over his sixgun and cocked it, dropped the hat back atop his head and scarcely breathed as that shadow seemed to float rather than crawl about two yards in front of him working through the underbrush without a sound.

It was rewarding to realise that all his waiting had not been in vain, and his judgment of the cowman had been correct: Garn had never intended to flee on horseback, he had intended to do precisely what Oliver had thought he'd do, try to get over against the eastward barranca and sneak along it until he could see up the trail where the gunshots had come from that had routed him back in the cache-clearing.

Respect for an enemy was always wise. For this particular enemy, who might believe he was going up against more than one man, the respect had to be great.

Oliver did not take his eyes off the shadow until it vanished beyond his sight near the rattlesnake den. Then he saw the man who had cast it before him. He was indeed crawling on all fours. His profile showed a jaw of granite, an attitude of fearless resolve, and a crafty expression.

Oliver scarcely breathed as Garn swung his head to the right, then to the left, paused in plain sight for a moment than positioned himself for more crawling.

Oliver waited until he could not miss and did not have to raise his voice. "Don't move. Don't even blink. Keep both hands out front like they are."

Frank Garn's back arched in surprise and despite Oliver's admonition he swung his head in the direction from which the voice had come.

Oliver did not give him a chance to recover from shock nor think about resisting. He gave another order: "Reach back with your right hand, pull out the gun and toss it."

Garn did not move.

Oliver eased down the hammer of his weapon, then cocked it again, this time with nothing to mask the sound. Garn was still squinting to find the body that owned Oliver's voice. If he had been flat on the ground he probably would have been successful, but from higher up there was too much intervening underbrush.

"The clock's tickin'," Oliver said and when the burly cowman still did not move, Oliver spoke again. "I'd as soon gut-shoot you as look at you. You got five seconds."

"Who are you? What's your problem with me?"

"Three seconds. Mister, I never bluff."

Frank Garn shifted his weight a little, plucked out his sixgun and tossed it aside, then he rocked back on his heels and spoke again. "Hell, I know who you are. You're the feller we never found up on the plateau, the feller whose horse no one could account for."

"Lie flat on your belly with both hands shoved out ahead as far as you can reach."

Garn leaned to obey. Oliver waited until he was in that belly-down position, then arose and shoved aside underbrush until he was standing above the cowman. Garn twisted his head and scowled. "Ain't that who you are?" he asked.

Oliver did not enlighten him. He put up his weapon and wagged his head. Frank Garn had caused him more discomfort than that damned posse up north, or anyone else for that matter. But — what could he do with him? As far as Oliver knew Garn hadn't broken the law, unless it was the law of common decency, and book law didn't hang anyone for that. In fact in maybe eight out of ten cases the book-lawmen admired someone who could steal and not break their law.

He ordered Garn to stand up, which the cowman did, and leaned to beat dust and tiny leaves off himself and, without any warning, hurled himself straight at Oliver.

The onslaught was too fast. The best Oliver could manage was to throw up an arm, but that wasn't good enough as the cowman's solid heft hit him head-on, almost knocked him to the ground, and punched half the breath out of him.

Garn was unhurt by the impact. He slashed at Oliver's face with a sidelong strike. It missed the cheek but tore up past the temple to send Oliver's hat sailing.

Garn was grunting as he came in on legs of spring steel. His face was contorted, the eyes glittering, the mouth open for huge amounts of air.

Oliver got away by half jumping, half twisting. Garn shot past him and came around on one leg. Oliver had one moment to decide he'd never faced anyone like Frank Garn before, and to understand that unless a miracle occurred, he was probably going to die right here in the scrub brush of a hidden canyon.

Garn was snarling like a wolf as he bore down on Oliver again, but this time balancing on his toes, expecting Oliver to elude him again by going sideways. Instead, Oliver gave ground in a rearward direction to encourage Garn to charge him. When the furious cowman took the bait and rushed, Oliver sidled to his right and kept sidling.

Garn swore at him and managed to check his rush and whirl. He had to reach Oliver before Oliver reached for his gun.

Garn was amazingly fast for a man of his burly build. Despite Oliver's speed at drawing the sixgun, Garn was on him before he could tilt it. He struck Oliver over the heart with a bone-chilling blow, then crossed up to aim for his jaw as

Oliver stumbled backwards. The second strike missed otherwise the fight would have ended then and there.

Garn continued to rush in, swinging and roaring curses like a madman. Oliver forced his battered body to respond in defence.

He shuffled clear, feinted left and right, saw Garn coming again and dropped to both knees as their bodies collided, but this time Frank Garn's momentum carried him in a high tumble over Oliver and flat down in a mount of rocks which were scattered every whichway when Garn landed among them.

As Oliver turned to draw, the rattling started. He stood transfixed as six large timber-rattlers came boiling out of their shattered den. Three of them coiled and struck almost simultaneously. The other three were slithering closer to the man scrambling to arise from the rocks.

Garn slipped and rolled sideways. The rocks were round and loose. He rolled directly over one snake into the face of the next one.

It struck him in the chest.

Oliver shot two snakes and kicked one to death which had slithered too close to his legs to fire at. He scuffed dust into the lidless eyes of another snake then shot it too.

Altogether, he killed five rattlesnakes. One disappeared into the underbrush, and when Oliver leaned to pull Garn out of the den by the ankles, three more emerged from among the rocks. He killed one of them with a rock and let the others glide away.

Garn was breathing hard, dripping sweat and glassy-eyed as Oliver helped him to arise and half guided, half dragged him away from the rattlesnake den. Where they finally halted Garn looked down at puncture marks in his body and said, "Gawd," in a horrified cry.

Oliver let him slide to the ground. The long silence after the furious gunfire had evidently been too much for the people hiding over by the thicket-camp. Several voices were raised. Oliver called back that it was safe for them to come out where he and Frank Garn were, then he refused to respond to any additional calls as he went to work on Garn, whose time was short at best and would very likely be even shorter than it would normally have been because he had been bitten more than once and because he had been excited, with his blood pounding, when he'd been struck.

11

A Night To Remember

GARN was glassy-eyed but his body was no longer tense and his breathing had lost most of its noisy gustiness as Oliver knelt to cut away his shirt and slit his trousers where there were the two tell-tale puncture marks of a poisonous snake. Not a word passed between them until Oliver rocked back on his heels to gaze at the cowman.

Garn was sweating. He said, "You knew that den was there, didn't you?"

Oliver was slow responding. Yes, he had known, but it had not once crossed his mind that someone might fall into it. "If you think I let you get down there, you're wrong."

"Who are you?"

"Oliver Dunhill. From up north. I

stumbled onto the Lees and heard their story."

Garn closed his eyes for a moment, he was becoming more relaxed. When he opened his eyes he said, "Can you cut 'em open and squeeze the poison out?"

"I can try, but it's kind of late."

"Do it!"

Oliver honed his knife on a stone and leaned to lance the puncture marks on Garn's chest. Without looking at the man he warned him that what he was going to do would be painful. Garn did not reply.

Oliver made the pair of cuts, encouraged the blood to well up and gently wagged his head as Garn said, "Keep pumping. How many times did they get me?"

"Four times, I think."

"Get on with it. What're you waitin' for?"

Oliver sat back, eyeing the cowman's face, which was beginning to get high colour. "Pardner," he told the injured man, "save your blood. It's not goin' to help if I cut the other places."

Garn glared. "You got me, ain't you?"

"Got you?"

"Yeah. You know about the will an' the deed. The Lees told you, an' now you can let me die and take over yourself."

Oliver fished for the makings, rolled and lit a smoke and gazed at the cowman. "I don't want anyone's ranch. As for lettin' you die, there's not a livin' soul could prevent it an' I think you know it. Tell me somethin', Mister Garn; why? You could've gone right on runnin' the place. You could have gone on ramrodding the place until you died of old age."

"It's not the same as ownin' a ranch, is it, cowboy? Ownin' is what every one of us wants, you included."

"No, not me included. Why didn't you try to buy 'em out? They likely would have sold to you."

"Why should I buy what I spent the best years of my life buildin' up? Specially after the old man's mind commenced slippin' and all. I ran the whole outfit, cowboy. I was the boss. I'd

163

done more to keep the place together an' prospering . . . "

"What's the matter?"

"A sort of grey film come over my eyes, then went back up. You got any whiskey?"

"No. Wish I did have though. By the way, those two fellers you think are livestock buyers — are deputy US marshals."

"You're crazy!"

"No. If you'd searched 'em you'd have found the badges."

Garn closed his eyes again. This time, during the interim, Oliver heard people moving in his direction through the underbrush. He arose to flex cramped muscles, looked around, could see very little because of the brush, and stood looking down as Garn said, "I never been so tired before." He did not open his eyes and Oliver did not comment on what he knew he was watching. "I come close though." Suddenly his eyes sprang wide open. "You're the one robbed that cache, ain't you?"

Oliver nodded.

"An' that measly Charley Hunter helped you, didn't he?"

Again Oliver nodded. The sound of people approaching was getting louder. Abruptly, one of the big federal officers burst into the tiny clearing. He had blood on a cheek from a thorn as he eyed Oliver first, then moved forward where he could see Frank Garn. "Shot?" he asked.

Oliver leaned to point to the wounds which were beginning to get a splotchy violet colour and which were swelling. "He fell into a snake den. Some of 'em came boilin' out fightin' mad and hit him."

"How many times?"

"Four times as far as I know."

The big lawman eyed Oliver again, then went to kneel beside Frank Garn as he said, "Can you hear me?" Garn gave no sign of it so the big man reached and gently shook him. "Listen to me, Garn. Can you hear me?"

From the opposite side of the thicket a wispy, sinewy man appeared, scratched, shirt torn, but unmindful of these things as he approached the downed man, leaned, screwed up his face and straightened up very slowly, looking squarely at Oliver. "You could blow a bugle in his ear an' he couldn't hear you."

Oliver eyed the wiry man. "I told you to stay up yonder undercover."

The sinewy man made a lopsided smile. "You did for a fact, but after all that gunfire I just plain had to know which one of you was still standin' up, if either of you was."

One of the lawmen eyed the older, smaller individual. "What'd you do with the papers you took out of Lee's hole in the ground?"

Charley Hunter smiled broadly when he replied. "You're talkin' to the wrong man, *amigo*. It wasn't me took them papers."

Oliver met the large man's steady gaze. "I got 'em, an' I'm goin' to keep 'em until the Lees get out here, then they can have 'em an' I'll ride on."

The pair of federal officers stood gazing

at Oliver until Walt and Annabelle Lee came into the clearing, stopped stone-still and remained that way staring at Frank Garn as Oliver told them what had happened. He could have told them more but he didn't, not until Garn's remaining pair of riders came up and the lanky one, who still showed signs of his encounter with Oliver, breathed a startled curse at the sight of Frank Garn, whose features were now made different by the increasing puffiness of his face. When the lanky man gasped Oliver tapped him with a stiff finger. "You'n your friend pick him up and pack him back to that camp where the cache was."

The lanky man didn't move. He was regarding Garn as though he were a leper. The other cowboy, however, leaned to grasp Garn under the arms and growled for his friend to pick up his feet.

The cavalcade made its way back to the cache-clearing where Garn was placed close while a fire was being worried into existence. Charley Hunter went foraging and returned with enough food to make a decent meal. As he was taking over tending the fire from Oliver Dunhill, Frank Garn sat straight up, looked around with wildly feverish eyes, saw Annabelle and said, "He's got the papers. He's fixin' to steal 'em from you," and collapsed. Walt caught the dying man, eased him gently down and blew out an unsteady breath.

They were all silent and solemn as they watched Garn die. It was not a spectacular passing; he simply let his eyes roll far back, turned loose all over and after a minute or so of difficult breathing, stopped breathing altogether.

The pair of lawmen helped Charley at the fire. Oliver jerked his head for Annabelle to follow him, and walked out of the clearing southward to the place where Hunter's horse had been tethered. There, he handed over the deed and her uncle's will. Back in camp two garrulous individuals got into a warm discussion about who was going to take the livestock to the creek to be watered, then off-saddled and hobbled for the night.

Annabelle and Oliver ignored this and everything else as she stood gazing at the papers in her hand. "How did you find them?"

"I didn't," he told her, and related what he knew of Charley Hunter and his ability to find things like caches. She put the papers into a pocket and avoided eye-contact with Oliver when she spoke again. "If I'd been in Garn's boots I wouldn't have done it. Owning something wouldn't be that important to me. Especially land."

Oliver's eyes had an ironic twinkle which she did not see when he replied, "Maybe you wouldn't, but I got a hunch that maybe two-thirds of all the fightin' that's ever gone on has been over land." Then he became more specific. "You can go back now. Go home, get settled in and commence ranching. There are worse ways of makin' a living."

"What about Frank Garn?"

Oliver shrugged. "Bury him. There's

no point in haulin' his carcass back to your ranch or to some town. Annabelle, a dead man is just that an' nothin' more an' in Garn's case maybe even a little less."

She looked squarely at him. "Right here? In this canyon?"

"Yes'm. But since we got no diggin' tools we'll bury him under a cairn the way they usually do it in places where the ground's too hard for digging."

She stood irresolutely gazing at the creek with her back to him. After a long time she said, "And you . . . ?"

"I was ridin' when I came into this canyon an' I'll be ridin' when I go out of it."

"What about those federal officers?"

He smiled at her back and carefully combed his beard with bent fingers. "It's been up to them, girl, from the time we met in the rattlesnake-clearing. I reckon whiskers make a difference."

She faced around. "Will you tell me the truth about something?"

"Yes'm."

"Did you rob a bank of nine thousand dollars?"

"Yes'm."

Silence settled between them. Annabelle had nothing more to say. She could think of nothing more to say. Oliver let the silence run on but when she simply stood there, hands clasped in front, gazing at him, her muteness clear evidence that she was not going to break the silence, he finally spoke.

"I don't have any excuse for doin' that except that I'd been unable to hire on for a full season an' was down to my last pinch of salt an' my last silver dollar for carbine shells to keep me in small game, when the idea struck me."

"You'd robbed banks before, Oliver?"

"No ma'm. That one was my first. It was touch an go for a while too. They chased me night an' day. They'd have got me too if I hadn't had a better horse than any of them had."

"Do you still have the money?"

He nodded and tapped his middle. "Next to my hide."

"Oliver."

"What."

"If you gave it back would the marshals let you go?"

"I doubt it, Annabelle. That's not how the law works. You can give things back until hell freezes over but you still got to stand trial for breakin' the law. That's what matters to fee-lawyers and the like. Breakin' the law. Not bein' willin' to give the loot back and sayin' you made a mistake." He paused, heard someone calling to them to come eat, and stepped close as he said, "I better ride out tonight. I need that much head-start." He smiled, tipped her face gently and kissed her squarely on the lips.

12

The Beginning of the End

BUT the opportunity to ride out did not materialise. They sat in a glum group, ate in silence and afterwards when some of the men lit up and relaxed the pair of lawmen showed interest in Oliver. They asked questions, some of which were harmless, some of which were not, and as he talked with them he knew exactly what they were doing.

Somehow, they'd become suspicious of him even though his appearance did not fit the likeness on the wanted dodger in their possession. He thought it was simply their nature to be suspicious of people, and was therefore very careful with his answers.

When Annabelle and her brother went off to their bedrolls and Garn's two cohorts, the lanky man and the one with a faint accent, also went out into the darkness to bed down, neither of the lawmen nor Charley Hunter showed any inclination to follow that example.

The older lawman spun a tedious tale of being on a manhunting trail, his eyes never leaving Oliver's face as he talked. His companion rolled and lit a smoke, offering the makings around, got no takers and shoved them back into a pocket. He seemed disinterested in what was going on, but that was an illusion. He and the older lawman had moved away from the others after Oliver and Annabelle had walked away, had talked a long time, and had then returned to join everyone in the meal, silent and thoughtful.

It was the wiry rangeman, Charley Hunter, who finally got things into focus by saying, "Well now, Marshal, years back when I rode for the army I done some manhuntin' too. Mostly for reservation-jumpers, but for other fellers as well, an' mostly I was beyond where there was any book-law." Charley paused to turn aside and expectorate, then smiled slightly as he turned back with his gaze fixed on the big lawman. "Sometimes I brought 'em back an' sometimes they just never made it back, but Mister Clavenger, I was damned sure who they was."

The large man was stuffing his pipe and replied without looking at Charley Hunter. "Sure about what?"

Charley snorted. "I told you. I been through this before. You'n your partner got suspicions about Mister Dunhill. But you got to be sure."

The younger man challenged that. "Why?"

Charley smiled at him. "Because there's the girl an' her brother, and us riders, that's why. You string him up an' if you can't prove he's an outlaw, a lot of folks are goin' to raise hell an' prop it up."

Marshal Clavenger got his pipe fired up. While working up a sustaining fire he eyed wizened Charley Hunter from an expressionless face. "Nobody's goin' to get strung up." His eyes regarded the cowboy coldly. "That's where professional lawmen differ from head-hunters, friend." He paused to puff up smoke then shifted his attention to Oliver, whose interest in all this had been increasing during that particular exchange between Hunter and the big lawman. For a while Clavenger smoked in silence, then he removed the pipe to ask a question. "What bothers me, Mister Dunhill, is your name. I never ran across a man who kept the same name if he had reason not to."

Oliver smiled straight back at the big, older man. "Dunhill's a fairly common name, Marshal."

Clavenger and his partner exchanged a glance before the older man spoke again. "Yeah, maybe it is, but we been on this particular trail since last fall, an' in the few places where we asked around, that name came up every blessed time." Clavenger gave up on keeping the pipe going and knocked it empty against a boot-heel. The younger deputy marshal, Les Moore, took it up by saying, "Where I'm havin' trouble, Mister Dunhill, is this here mess where you took on that feller Garn an' his friends, got the deed an' the will, and gave it to the girl an' her brother."

"Why should that cause you trouble?" Oliver asked, and got a blunt reply.

"Only outlaw I ever heard of who did things like that was a feller named Robin Hood, and that's a long time ago."

Oliver laughed. "I don't know anythin' about that feller, Mister Moore, but I suspect just anyone, includin' Charley Hunter here an' maybe his friends, wouldn't like what Frank Garn tried to do. How about you; would you approve of it?"

Moore did not answer; he sighed, shoved up to his feet, grumbled something about being tired to the bone, and shuffled away from the fire. Marshal Clavenger continued to sit and gaze into the dying fire. Eventually, when Charley Hunter also walked out into the darkness Clavenger raised his eyes to Oliver. "I'm goin' to bed down out among the horses, Mister Dunhill." He continued to gaze at Oliver a few more moments, then arose and left the fire.

Oliver sighed. They were reasonably certain about him, and to be doubly certain they would make sure he didn't slip away in the night.

He could have tried it anyway. He had proved his adeptness at moving soundlessly. He looked over at the blanket-covered mound where Frank Garn was lying, decided he was just too damned tired to try it tonight after all, and went in search of his blankets.

It was probably a good thing he didn't try it because while the older lawman was out with the horses his young companion only fitfully slept, otherwise he watched Oliver.

In the morning Hunter and his companions from the cow outfit were stirring up the fire, ready to make another meal, when Oliver awakened. Charley looked out there, watched Oliver roll out and shook his head. He would have bet a hatful of new money, if he'd had it, that Oliver would be nowhere around come sun-up. He was plainly disgusted that he was.

The men carried Garn out a ways and worked for two hours piling rocks on him. By the time they were ready to strike camp Annabelle had got involved in a long discussion with Marshal Clavenger. From her expression when the others returned from building the stone cairn, she hadn't succeeded in her mission, which had simply been to plead for Oliver.

Clavenger was not rude to her, he was simply unmovable.

The sun was climbing as they struck out northward toward the east-side barranca with the trail leading up out of Horse Canyon. There was very little conversation, but evidently the pair of lawmen had talked earlier among themselves, because while the younger lawman led the way up the canyon, the older one brought up the drag where he could watch everyone up ahead.

Oliver rode with Walt Lee, who was glum and not very talkative. The cavalcade made steady progress under increasing heat but without hurrying. Their animals had been on grass and browse, which would sustain them for a long walk, but not for anything faster.

They were passing the place where Oliver'd had his camp when Annabelle came up beside him and smiled, not encouragingly but rather wistfully. He smiled back. "Maybe you could keep Hunter and the two other riders," he said to her. "They were fools, not really bad. Everyone's a fool some of the time, Annabelle, some more than others. What counts with men like Hunter is that they're loyal. They worked for Garn. He was their boss an' their brains. I think if you give them a chance they'll be just as loyal to you."

She let him get it all said before speaking. "It'll be up to them. We'll keep them if they want to stay. What about you?"

"Well," he replied quietly while ranging

a long look up where the young lawman was slouching along, "somewhere between here an' wherever they figure to go, if they want me to go with 'em, I expect there'll be some dust an' smoke."

She bit her lip, faced forward and rode past his camp without saying a word.

The lead rider raised his arm for a halt when they were within sight of the trail leading up out of the canyon. It was a pretty fair climb. He swung off and said they'd rest the horses before starting up.

Marshal Clavenger rode toward the front of the little column without once looking at the Lees or Oliver Dunhill. Up where he swung to the ground near his partner, there was a brief conversation, then both men squatted in meagre shade. The other riders took their cue from this and also got settled for a rest. But a situation which had been developing now since last evening was made clear in the way the HL riders grouped around the Lees and Oliver, leaving the pair of federal lawmen up ahead by themselves.

The lanky cowboy Oliver had knocked senseless and who still showed bruises, leaned and said, "We can keep between them an' you; keep 'em from goin' after you."

Oliver smiled at the man. "You most likely could, and they'd arrest all of you."

Hunter snorted. "That wouldn't be a real wise thing for 'em to try, Mister Dunhill."

Oliver considered the three rangeriders. Yesterday their loyalty to the man under the pile of rocks back yonder would have encouraged them to try and kill him. Today the same sense of loyalty had been transferred to Oliver and the Lees.

He shook his head at them. "You boys got a real knack for bein' on the wrong side. You start a fight with those federal deputies an' even if they don't kill you, you'll spend the rest of your lives hidin' from the law. Not cow-town law, federal law."

Charley would have argued but Oliver waved that off as he stood up and turned his back on them to take Annabelle by the hand and lead her out a ways. Where they stopped he said, "Are you goin' to keep the ranch an' run it, or sell out an' go back east?"

"Keep it . . . Oliver, I asked Marshal Clavenger if you gave back the money would he let you go."

Oliver stared at her. If she'd said that to Clavenger it was the same as admitting that he was their outlaw, and worse, that she knew he was. He twisted to glance up where the pair of lawmen were coming up off the ground to snug up their cinches. She spoke again, "Will they take you back up north?"

He nodded, eyeing her dispassionately. She had meant well and someday it would probably occur to her that she had delivered him into the hands of the lawmen, but right now she was too distraught to think clearly. "Keep the place," he told her, "and someday I'll come ridin' down the lane."

Tears blurred her vision.

Clavenger called for everyone to mount up. He was already in the saddle, was reining back to let them all pass by so he could take his position in the drag again.

The horses were rested. They'd picked a little grass, had tanked up at the creek, were ready for the climb. As the Lees rode past Marshal Clavenger they both looked directly at him from bitter faces. He ignored that, waited for everyone to pass then spoke to Oliver as he was passing. "I'm not real happy about this, but you took the chance and I took an oath years back."

Oliver nodded.

The big lawman held up a hand for Oliver to halt. The others were moving up ahead and did not see any of this. Clavenger held his hand out, palm up. "Your gun," he said.

Oliver reined to a halt. "You haven't charged me with anything."

"Didn't have anything solid to charge you *with* until I talked to the girl. Your gun!"

Up ahead where the younger deputy was already fifty or sixty feet up the trail his horse suddenly squalled and reared. Because the animal was already moving uphill the same rearing action which wouldn't have been particularly hazardous in flat country, became extremely dangerous on the slope. The animal lost its balance and went over backwards.

Deputy Les Moore, wedged between the fork and the cantle, kicked his feet free but had no time to brace one hand on the fork and shove sideways. The horse had caught him completely unprepared. It crashed backwards, panicking the horses farther down the trail who tried to spin and get back down to level ground, with a resulting pandemonium that froze Clavenger and Oliver in their tracks.

Because of the billowing dust and the writhing horse on its back who was making more dust, it was impossible to see what exactly had happened up there, but Charley Hunter sprang to the ground and made a bow-legged dash up to where the entangled lawman and his threshing animal were struggling.

Oliver spun his horse and hooked him into a leaping-out run. He passed them all, flung off and ran up the trail where Charley Hunter was swearing at the top of his voice as he tried to catch the flying reins of the downed horse. He caught them finally, and yanked the horse's head around so that it could scramble to its feet.

The horse was wild-eyed, its sides heaving, quivering from head to rump as Charley tried to lead it down the trail. It planted all four legs and refused to budge until Oliver got around it and ran full tilt into its haunches, forcing the horse to get un-tracked.

Charley bellowed angrily at the men who were coming up the narrow trail. He gestured wildly for them to go back, which they did because otherwise Hunter could not have got the horse back down to flat country.

Oliver grabbed the inert bulk of the younger lawman, got him back onto the trail, pushed him around until his head was uphill, then fished out his blue bandana and wiped caked sweat and dust off the deputy's face. He was unconscious, his face was ashen, his breathing was laboured, and although his eyelids flickered that could have been a bad sign instead of a good one.

Oliver had his shirt open by the time Marshal Clavenger got up there. The bruise was unmistakable. When a horse went up and over and the rider could not shove sideways, eight out of ten times the saddlehorn with all the animal's weight behind it, came down in the middle of the man's chest, directly over the breastbone and the heart.

Kicking horses could injure, even cripple people, and biting horses could take a finger off, but those kinds of horses rarely killed anyone. An up-and-over horse would almost invariably kill its rider if he hadn't gotten far enough to one side as the animal came down to avoid a crushed breastbone.

13

The Meeting at the Creek

THEY carried Deputy Moore back into tree-shade near the creek. There was almost no talk as they laid him out until Charley Hunter growled for one of his companions to examine the frightened animal for injuries, then jerked his head for Oliver to accompany him and went trudging grimly back up the trail.

When they were out of earshot of the others Charley said, "Now's your chance. There's just the big one. We can keep him settin' down there until the cows come home."

Oliver did not respond. He hiked up where the horse had reared and quartered for something he didn't see, but which Charley Hunter pointed out with a sigh as he said, "Has this canyon got a name, you reckon?"

"Horse Canyon, more'n likely. Mustangs water and graze down here. Why?"

"Look yonder, north of where the ruckus started. See that smooth place that looks like someone'd dragged a rope? Now then, look across the trail where that same sign shows again." Charley looked at Oliver. "It may be Horse Canyon, Mister Dunhill, but them marks was made by a big rattlesnake." Charley paused to wag his head and expectorate. "It ought to be called Rattlesnake Canyon. That's what spooked the horse; darned few horses wouldn't have gone crazy with a rattlesnake underfoot."

Oliver was studying the sign when a calm, deep voice spoke behind him as Marshal Clavenger said, "What was it?" Oliver pointed and the big man leaned to look, then straightened back slowly as Charley Hunter started back toward treeshade where the others were standing around Deputy Moore.

Clavenger squinted at the location of the sun, tipped down his hat and gazed at Oliver. "You believe in omens?" he asked.

Oliver believed in what his eyes told him. "I believe in rattlesnakes an' this place has more'n its share of them. First Garn, now your deputy."

Clavenger inclined his head. "That's what I mean. Have you ever had the feelin' you're buckin' fate?"

Oliver studied the large man's face. Clavenger was dead serious. "Never thought much about it, Marshal."

"I have. Many times. Maybe in my business a man has more time to wonder about such things."

"Maybe. What's on your mind?"

"Lookin' at things my way, Mister Dunhill, Frank Garn never should have come back down into this canyon. If he hadn't, by now he'd be alive. But he came back, and whatever's got a hand in folks' affairs decided he wasn't ever goin' to learn, and you know the rest. He's still down here. He'll be down here forever. Rattlesnakes, Mister Dunhill."

Oliver was faintly frowning at the big, older man. He'd known superstitious people, lots of them, but Howard Clavenger was the last man he'd have thought might be like that. He was big and confident, calm and thoughtful. If there was a nerve in his carcass it didn't show.

Oliver said, "How's your deputy?"

"Bad off."

"Busted breastbone?"

"No, I don't think so. He must have been off-balance in the saddle when the horse went up, and maybe that pushed him a little more off-centre. That bruise looks like hell but it goes around on his left side over the ribs. I'd say he wasn't sittin' square up in the saddle or he'd be dead." Clavenger stopped speaking and stared at Oliver, who took a chance and said, "Omen, Mister Clavenger?"

The big man smiled without a shred of humour. He moved past Oliver to lead the way back down where the others had made camp within walking distance of the creek where the heat could not quite reach them, when it came along later in the day.

Deputy Moore was conscious. Anabelle had removed his shirt and was bathing his feverish face with wet rags while the others stood watching, solemn as a clutch of owls.

Everything had changed. Even the way the men spoke to each other was different. The attitude was now that of people in a strange place who had formerly had little in common except distrust of one another, but who were now seemingly uneasy about this isolated, distant canyon and ganging together in a vague kind of uneasy fear.

When Oliver and the large lawman walked up Annabelle leaned back to look up, not at Clavenger, at Oliver. He winked at her but otherwise showed no expression as he sank to one knee in the shade beside the injured lawman.

Oliver studied the swelling which was more off-centre than he'd expected it to be, and was turning a splotchy shade of angry purple. Deputy Moore grimaced.

Oliver said, "Take a deep breath," and the lawman scowled. "No thanks." Oliver nodded. "Busted ribs?"

"Yep. Feels like everything's busted."

Oliver sighed, shoved back his hat and said, "Spit."

The injured man made the effort. It cost him something but he expectorated and Oliver leaned to look, then straightened back as Deputy Moore said, "Blood?"

"No. Spit again."

The result was the same so Oliver smiled. "You're hung with horseshoes, partner."

Moore made a ghastly smile in return. "Sure don't feel like it, cowboy."

Oliver stood up as Annabelle moved in to raise Moore's head so he could drink. Again, it cost him, but he got the water down, then as she eased his head back down he let go with a shallow sigh and swung to look at Deputy Clavenger. "Made a mess of it, didn't I?"

Clavenger's answer was cryptic. "No. It's been a mess since we come onto these folks." He paused, groped for his little pipe and while stuffing it with shag he drily said, "Well, this isn't a place I'd pick to camp for a week or two, Les, but that's about the size of it. You won't be able to move for at least that long an' maybe a lot longer."

The big man knelt and gently probed the swollen place and wagged his head. "Two busted ribs," he announced, and fired up the little pipe as he remained on one knee gazing at his companion. "That clean pair of drawers in your saddlebag will do. It's goin' to be painful but you got to be lashed so the bones'll heal."

Deputy Moore let his gaze drift around at the solemn faces, and breathed a curse. "Damn!"

Clavenger spoke through a fragrant cloud of pipe smoke. "Didn't you see the rattlesnake?"

Moore's eyes widened on the older man. "Is that what caused it?"

"Yeah."

"No, I didn't see anything. Wasn't lookin' for anythin' except how steep the trail was up ahead. Howard?

Rattlesnakes?"

Clavenger solemnly inclined his head. "You remember what I told you about sometimes a man's just not supposed to do something?"

Moore's expression toughened. "You goin' to start on that again? Rattlesnakes are common. We've seen lots of 'em lately."

"That's my point, Les. Too many."

Clearly the younger lawman did not subscribe to his partner's superstition, or whatever it was. He looked away and saw Annabelle standing with the others. He smiled at her. "You got a little more water, ma'm?"

She turned toward the creek with the dented cooking-pan from her brother's pack. Oliver went with her. When they were beside the watercourse she said, "Is Mister Clavenger superstitious?"

"He sounds like he is."

"Well; so am I, Oliver. Isn't that a lot of coincidences — first Garn, then Mister Moore."

He didn't reply immediately because

he was beginning to think of his own encounters with snakes in Horse Canyon. She took his silence as scepticism and knelt to fill the pan with water, speaking while her back was to him. "Both times someone ran into trouble when they were going to make trouble for you."

He shoved his hat back, sank to the grass beside her and chuckled. "Well now, if a man's got such a thing as a guardian angel, I sure don't feel real flattered if mine is a rattlesnake."

She put the pan between them in the grass, leaned to drink, and reared back using a sleeve to dry her face before she said, "Mister Clavenger won't leave his deputy. No one else will try to stop you."

He nodded about that. "Trouble is, I've been riding back-trails long enough. Sure, I can ride out of here, but all that'll buy me is maybe a month. Annabelle, the federal law never lets up. Like I told you, Annabelle, the federal law never quits."

"You could change your name, keep

your beard, go so far away they'd never find you."

He gently shook his head at her. "I just told you, the federals never let up. They'd show up someday, somewhere. It's not like county lawmen who got no authority outside their bailiwicks. Federal marshals got jurisdiction from one end of the country to the other end."

She got a vertical line between her eyes. "Oliver, are you going to let them take you back, send you to prison?"

He had no chance to answer because Marshal Clavenger appeared behind them clearing his throat to let them know he was there.

Oliver stood up and offered Annabelle his hand so she too could arise. She was holding the pan of water when Clavenger said, "He's mighty thirsty, young lady."

She looked from one man to the other one, then walked briskly back the way she had come leaving Marshal Clavenger puffing on his pipe as he studied Oliver Dunhill. He removed the pipe, knocked it empty, pocketed it and spoke quietly. "He can't move for a while. Maybe a couple of weeks, maybe a full month, an' even when he can set his horse, it's goin' to be darned uncomfortable."

Oliver nodded in agreement.

"Mister Dunhill, let's talk straight out. All right with you?"

"Yes."

"Well then tell me — how much of that nine thousand you still got?"

"All but about a hundred dollars of it. I had to get my horse re-shod, I had to buy more grub, had to lie over a time or two."

"You got it cached down in here somewhere, or maybe up your backtrail?"

Oliver shook his head, meeting the large man's gaze without blinking. "I got it in a buckskin belt around my middle."

That did not appear to surprise the lawman. "I been speculatin' a little."

"About rattlesnakes, Marshal?"

Clavenger's eyes showed an ironic twinkle. "Sort of, maybe, in a way. The girl talked herself blue in the face tellin' me you'd give back the money if I'd leave you alone."

"Yeah. She told me. She also told me you wouldn't budge."

"Well now, Mister Dunhill, I need another honest answer from you. How many banks or stages have you robbed?"

"None. That was my first, an' I guess my last, hold-up. You got a dodger about me?"

"Yes."

"Does it say I've robbed before?"

"No. Why in hell did you do it?"

"Because I was broke, gettin' hungry, couldn't find a ridin' job — and because I was a damned fool."

Clavenger shoved both hands into trouser pockets and gazed at the busy little creek for a moment before speaking again. "You want to give the money back, Mister Dunhill?"

"Yes."

Clavenger made a little gesture. "You're not a real rousin' success as an outlaw. You got a beard an' the likeness of you on my dodger don't show that. But it does mention somethin' else. That fancy gun you wear."

Oliver accepted that without surprise. "I should have ditched it, I guess. The reason I didn't was because it belonged to a partner of mine who died after a stampede went over him in Wyoming. We was real close."

Clavenger nodded slightly, raised his head and while looking Oliver in the eyes, said, "You'd never make an outlaw. You're carryin' a gun that attracts attention, because you couldn't bear to toss it down a canyon because it reminded you of someone. An' you busted into that mess between Frank Garn and the Lees. An' you worried about my deputy back there. Mister Dunhill, I got to ride back out of this damned canyon when Les is able to ride again. You know there's more snakes down here. Me an' Les takin' you out of here — I just plain don't think we're supposed to do that an' I don't want to put it to a test. Dyin' with your carcass full of venom is a pretty terrible way to die."

Oliver's brows drew inward as he studied the large man. "An' if I hand over the money-belt, Marshal . . . ?"

"An' give me your word about doin' anythin' like that again."

Oliver unbuttoned his shirt, untied the buckskin belt, pulled it out and handed it to the big man, still looking sceptical. As he was stuffing his shirt back inside his britches he said, "What about your oath, Marshal?"

Clavenger was carefully folding the money-belt when he replied. "My oath don't require me to get myself or my partner killed." He stuffed the belt into a pocket and raised his slaty eyes. "If what we can accomplish will set things to rights. All they want back up in Montana is their money back. All Les an' I want is to be able to ride out of this damned canyon an' never see it again. You ready to give me your word?"

"Yes sir. You got it, but even if I didn't give it to you I can tell you for a fact outlawin' isn't for me."

Clavenger reached over to roughly slap the younger man on the shoulder. "This is just between you'n me. You understand?"

"Yes."

"All right. While there's still daylight you go on back, help the girl an' her brother rig out, take those mangy rangemen with you an' ride up out of here."

"You'll need grub, Marshal. A month is a long time in one camp."

"Never mind. You just ride up out of here an' take them with you. That's all you got to do. Les an' I'll make out. We been in bad places before. As bad as this."

"An' what do I tell Annabelle and the others?"

"Whatever you want to tell 'em. For openers, you don't look like the man on our wanted poster. An' her — well — someday you can tell her you gave the money back. And Mister Dunhill, when you lead 'em up out of here, for Chris'sake watch out for rattlesnakes."

14

" . . . Will I Do?"

OLIVER could have waited until
morning but there was still
slightly more than half a day
left when he told Hunter and Walt Lee to
rig up, get the pair of Garn riders ready,
and with Les Moore watching but silent,
and Marshal Clavenger standing with his
horse, his back to the others, although
questions hung in the air almost solid
enough to touch, no one spoke as Oliver
set the example by rigging out his mule-
nosed bay horse.

Only when he swung into the saddle
waiting for the others, did Marshal
Clavenger turn and almost imperceptibly
nod his head.

Oliver leaned to smile at the injured
man and said, "Take care, partner," then
straightened in the saddle and led off

in the direction of the same trail where Deputy Moore'd had his accident.

None of the riders spoke as they started up the trail. Charley Hunter set an example for his companions; he let his animal move on a loose rein while Charley sat slightly off-centre watching the trail like a hawk.

Oliver, with Annabelle directly behind him, neither looked around nor spoke. He concentrated on reaching the top-out. When he got up there and turned his horse so its rump was to the north where a faint breeze was coming from, he watched the others break up over the rim one at a time, then turned southward to strike out again.

Annabelle let the others troop past for a long moment as she leaned to look back down where two horses were grazing near a bosque of shade trees. She could not see either of the lawmen. The reason she couldn't was because Marshal Clavenger was hunkering beneath the same old tree that was shading his companion. Clavenger was smoking his pipe and nodding slightly as Deputy Moore was speaking. Moore's voice was slightly husky and he paused often to take down a shallow breath, but his mind was as clear as glass as he said, "I'm not havin' any trouble with it, Howard. To be truthful, I just couldn't fit Dunhill into what I've come to have as a mental image of an outlaw. But we got to lie when we get back up north. Give 'em back the damned money an' lie."

Clavenger trickled smoke. "Why do we have to lie?"

"Because they're goin' to demand to know how we got the money without gettin' the man who took it."

Clavenger got more comfortable beneath the shielding leafy limbs of the big old tree. "When I was first startin' out I worked with a man named Tom Houston."

"I know. You've told me about him."

Clavenger went on as though there had been no interruption. "Lots of times when you're young you meet older men who give you advice and whatnot, an' later, when you're a lot older you find out that maybe half of what they told you wasn't right."

"You've told me this before, Howard."

Clavenger did as he'd done before, he turned a deaf ear as he puffed his pipe before speaking again. He was softly smiling and gazing across the creek toward the easterly barranca. "Tom told me a man never had to lie, he just didn't have to tell everything he knew." Clavenger dropped his gaze to the injured man, still softly smiling. "We found our fugitive, didn't we?"

"Yep."

"An' we caught him."

"Yep."

"An' we got the loot back from him, Les, then you got hurt an' while I was lookin' after you, he rode away. Rode up out of the canyon an' me bein' tied down by takin' care of you, we never saw him again."

Les raised the arm on the side of his body that wasn't painful and scratched a stubbly face. "An' that's not lying?"

"You got hurt, didn't you; an' I got to look after you, don't I; and he rode up out of here, didn't he?"

Moore eased the arm back to his side, wrinkled his brow at the older man and weakly shook his head a little. Someday he might figure out to his own satisfaction whether he'd been part of a secret conspiracy, and then again he might never figure it out because, as the years passed, the fine points would become blurred and ultimately unimportant. But right now he said, "Well, we got back the money anyway. Howard, what do we eat while we're down here — rattlesnakes?"

The big man arose, knocked his pipe empty and grinned as he went over to rummage among their saddlery for his saddlebags. "Not for a while we don't eat snake. There's game aplenty down here, I've seen lots of tracks. You want some more water?"

When Les Moore nodded and Clavenger moved away from the tree into plain sight from above on his way to the creek, Annabelle was already a mile down-country riding with the others so she didn't see him.

There was a slight wind atop the plateau. Unlike other times when the wind scourged this open country, this time the wind was gentler, it kept the heat from becoming unpleasant as the little party plodded southward, each with his, or her, own thoughts, right up until they dipped down into a wide arroyo and came up the far side to startle a band of wild horses who hung momentarily still, then whirled away in a dust-raising run and Charley Hunter called ahead to Oliver. "Couple hunnert dollars worth of horseflesh, Mister Dunhill."

Oliver looked back, nodded and kept right on riding. Annabelle rode with her brother until they crossed through a spit of trees and emerged upon a slight rise which overlooked miles of southerly grassland which was totally empty. She rode up beside Oliver, watched the way he was studying the lie of land and said, "Good livestock country?"

He nodded. "The best. If there's water."

She raised an arm. "Aren't those cottonwood trees?"

He saw them, recognised them as cottonwoods and gazed at her; he was not accustomed to tact but he knew it when he heard it, so he smiled. "All right. We'll camp there. How far is it to your ranch?"

She let the arm fall back to her side while replying. "In miles, I don't know. In days of riding, maybe fifteen or twenty." She looked quizzically at him. "Is that too long?"

"Too long for what?"

"Well, for you to stay with us."

"Annabelle . . . No, it's not too long." He looked back. The others were beyond hearing distance. "How many riders did your uncle keep?"

"Three riders and a range-boss."

"Well, Charley'd make you a good range-boss, I think."

"How about you?"

He looked away from her. "If your brother will ride that'd be one too many men. But I'd like to work for you."

She squinted at him. "What about all those things you told me about federal lawmen never sleeping, or something like that?"

"I gave the money to Marshal Clavenger."

"Will that be enough? You said — "

"We talked, Annabelle. We had quite a talk at the creek. That's why Clavenger didn't make a move as we rigged out and left."

"He won't come after you?"

"Not if his word is any good an' I think it is."

She blushed, which he did not notice because he was evening-up his reins. "You're hired." When he finally turned she was still blushing. He winked at her and led off down the far side of the low hill, riding in the direction of the cottonwoods.

She reined back to ride stirrup with her brother. He had watched her up ahead with Oliver and when she seemed

211

to have difficulty speaking Walt said, "Annabelle, you like him." It was not a question but rather a statement.

"Yes, I like him. Don't you?"

Walt rubbed the tip of his nose before replying. "Yeah, but maybe not in the same way."

She smiled guilelessly. "That's probably a healthy sign."

He scowled at her. "Is there somethin' you want to tell me?"

She was watching the bearded man up ahead riding easily along. "A lot of things. But someday, not right now . . . Walt?"

"What."

"I hired him on as a rider."

"Good."

She was relieved. Before she could speak again, though, her brother had something to add. "If he likes you the way you look now, Annabelle, wait until he sees you in clean clothes with your hair set and all."

He was teasing her, which she knew and accepted because this was something he'd always done, but she had to reply so

212

she said, "I don't know whether he likes me or not."

"Oh yes you do. Sis, I may not be much of a cowman because I haven't been around livestock that much, but I'm older'n you an' I've been around people a lot longer. Take my word for it, he's fond of you."

She refused to meet his gaze, rode along very erect in the saddle concentrating on the cottonwood grove, cheeks flushed. Walt smiled to himself, turned his attention ahead where Oliver was sitting his motionless horse looking at the grove. He turned and called back. "Water up there."

Charley Hunter the practical frontiersman drily called back, "That's nice. How about firewood? Cottonwood don't burn worth a darn unless it's bone dry, an' then it ain't the best."

Oliver rode in among the shaggy old trees, swung off where a marshy expanse of spongy earth overgrown with thistles and ripgut showed where the seepage spring ran a fair head of water, knelt with his back to the others to hobble his horse, then stood up to begin off-saddling. Behind him the others were doing the same thing.

The wind had died away. It was late afternoon with dusk on the way as they went about establishing camp. The rangemen did everything as instinctively as rangemen always did who have never lived much differently. The lanky man whose bruises still showed where he'd made the mistake of trying to whip Oliver, sauntered over, pulled off a worn old riding-glove and shoved out his hand as he said, "Mister Dunhill . . . "

Oliver turned, eyed the extended hand, gripped it and slapped the lanky man on the shoulder. Neither of them said another word, both of them turned back to help gather bone-grey dead firewood and Charley Hunter, trying to get a panful of water from the spring, turned the air blue when, despite all his caution, he sank to his ankles in mud.

They had a cooking-fire burning as dusk settled. They were hungry people,

214

but more than that they were tired people.

As they sat down to eat Oliver expected questions. He knew how curious they were. He'd led them out of Horse Canyon with two armed lawmen watching them go. They had a right to be curious but he said nothing and they asked no questions.

After supper the rangemen lingered briefly with Walt at the fire making desultory conversation until they headed for their soogans one at a time until Walt was left alone.

He gazed out where Oliver and his sister were going among the horses, ostensibly to look for saddle-sores or scratches, but actually simply to be close to each other. Walt sighed and told himself that someday, maybe not for a while but someday, he was going to bust right out and ask Oliver what exactly had happened back yonder. Unless of course Oliver volunteered that information before then.

The fire burned low, dusk arrived,

Walt followed the example of the other men and went over to his bedroll to lie on his back looking at the panoply of faint stars in their setting of infinity.

Out where Oliver and Annabelle were standing together the stars seemed brighter, the night air sweeter, and the silence everlasting as he said, "Did you tell your brother you'd hired me on?"

"Yes."

"What did he say?"

"Good."

"That's all?"

She blushed in the shadows, which he could not see. "Not exactly. We talked."

"Anything I should know?"

She smiled sweetly at him. "Not right now. Not tonight. But someday. The same as *you'll* explain things — someday."

He smiled at her. "Mind if I guess?"

"No."

"Well, more'n likely he said I was fond of you."

" . . . Yes."

"I figured your brother to be an

observant individual the first time we talked."

"Are you, Oliver?"

"Yes'm. More than just fond of you."

She moved close, stood on her tiptoes and kissed him lightly on the cheek. "That's my 'thank you' for taking our side back there."

He looked down at her. "You don't owe me anythin' for that."

"Well then, it was for something else," she said, and leaned a little.

He kissed her very gently on the lips. Her arms went up around his neck and an early moon came soaring into the velvety night.

Somewhere in the westerly distance a band of foraging coyotes paused in their nocturnal run to sound at the rising moon, and every other nocturnal animal that heard them, except those with wings such as night-hunting owls, ran for the safety of its burrow except for a solitary cougar who had missed mating in the springtime and was now moving restlessly in search of a female who might be interested. He halted to make his coughing call and his hair-raising scream, and that worked on the coyotes exactly as their sounding had worked on smaller animals. They raced down the night for a breathless mile, not because they feared being attacked by the mountain lion, whose normal diet did not include coyotes, but because instinct told them he was in his rut and would attack them now when he wouldn't even consider attacking them any other time.

When Annabelle flinched and stayed as close as she could get to Oliver, he said, "He's not going to do anything."

"Are you plumb sure of that?"

"Yes'm. He might make a run on the horses, but not when he can catch human scent."

He took her by the hand and walked northward a fair distance before halting when the big cat screamed again, sounding more distant this time. Oliver gauged the scream and considered the country where the lion was aiming for.

"Timber," he said softly. "He knows we're down here an' maybe he figured to come among the cottonwoods and ambush some critter who'd come for a drink, but not after he picked up man-scent, so now he's goin' north up where there's timber. That's his natural place anyway."

She looked at him. "How long have you been a rangeman?"

"Ever since I was a button an' ran away from a workhouse."

"No family, Oliver?"

"No. Not that I ever knew anyway."

She pulled him along by the hand, heading back in the direction of the cottonwood-camp. "Do you want to settle down?"

He smiled at her. "I've always wanted to settle in one place, have a stake in something."

"I'm glad. I've always wanted the same thing, but with a family."

He made no attempt to pursue this subject but when they were within sight of the shaggy old trees he said, "It's important for a person to belong, isn't it?"

"Yes. And to have someone who belongs to them." She halted and turned to face him.

He nodded solemnly. "An' to have someone who belongs to them, yes'm."

"Oliver . . . will I do?"

He was off-guard but recovered swiftly. "You'll do just fine."

"Then hold me."

He did, and so faint it was almost unheard, the big cat screamed again.

THE END

FIGHTING RAMROD
Charles N. Heckelmann

Most men would have cut their losses, but Frazer counted the bullets in his guns and said he'd soak the range in blood before he'd give up another inch of what was his.

LONE GUN
Eric Allen

Smoke Blackbird had been away too long. The Lequires had seized the Blackbird farm, forcing the Indians and settlers off, and no one seemed willing to fight! He had to fight alone.

THE THIRD RIDER
Barry Cord

Mel Rawlins wasn't going to let anything stand in his way. His father was murdered, his two brothers gone. Now Mel rode for vengeance.

ARIZONA DRIFTERS
W. C. Tuttle

When drifting Dutton and Lonnie Steelman decide to become partners they find that they have a common enemy in the formidable Thurston brothers.

TOMBSTONE
Matt Braun

Wells Fargo paid Luke Starbuck to outgun the silver-thieving stagecoach gang at Tombstone. Before long Luke can see the only thing bearing fruit in this eldorado will be the gallows tree.

HIGH BORDER RIDERS
Lee Floren

Buckshot McKee and Tortilla Joe cut the trail of a border tough who was running Mexican beef into Texas. They stopped the smuggler in his tracks.

BRETT RANDALL, GAMBLER
E. B. Mann

Larry Day had the choice of running away from the law or of assuming a dead man's place. No matter what he decided he was bound to end up dead.

THE GUNSHARP
William R. Cox

The Eggerleys weren't very smart. They trained their sights on Will Carney and Arizona's biggest blood bath began.

THE DEPUTY OF SAN RIANO
Lawrence A. Keating and
Al. P. Nelson

When a man fell dead from his horse, Ed Grant was spotted riding away from the scene. The deputy sheriff rode out after him and came up against everything from gunfire to dynamite.

FARGO: MASSACRE RIVER
John Benteen

The ambushers up ahead had now blocked the road. Fargo's convoy was a jumble, a perfect target for the insurgents' weapons!

SUNDANCE: DEATH IN THE LAVA
John Benteen

The Modoc's captured the wagon train and its cargo of gold. But now the halfbreed they called Sundance was going after it . . .

HARSH RECKONING
Phil Ketchum

Five years of keeping himself alive in a brutal prison had made Brand tough and careless about who he gunned down . . .

FARGO: PANAMA GOLD
John Benteen

With foreign money behind him, Buckner was going to destroy the Panama Canal before it could be completed. Fargo's job was to stop Buckner.

FARGO: THE SHARPSHOOTERS
John Benteen

The Canfield clan, thirty strong were raising hell in Texas. Fargo was tough enough to hold his own against the whole clan.

PISTOL LAW
Paul Evan Lehman

Lance Jones came back to Mustang for just one thing — revenge! Revenge on the people who had him thrown in jail.

HELL RIDERS
Steve Mensing

Wade Walker's kid brother, Duane, was locked up in the Silver City jail facing a rope at dawn. Wade was a ruthless outlaw, but he was smart, and he had vowed to have his brother out of jail before morning!

DESERT OF THE DAMNED
Nelson Nye

The law was after him for the murder of a marshal — a murder he didn't commit. Breen was after him for revenge — and Breen wouldn't stop at anything . . . blackmail, a frameup . . . or murder.

DAY OF THE COMANCHEROS
Steven C. Lawrence

Their very name struck terror into men's hearts — the Comancheros, a savage army of cutthroats who swept across Texas, leaving behind a blood-stained trail of robbery and murder.

SUNDANCE: SILENT ENEMY
John Benteen

A lone crazed Cheyenne was on a personal war path. They needed to pit one man against one crazed Indian. That man was Sundance.

LASSITER
Jack Slade

Lassiter wasn't the kind of man to listen to reason. Cross him once and he'll hold a grudge for years to come — if he let you live that long.

LAST STAGE TO GOMORRAH
Barry Cord

Jeff Carter, tough ex-riverboat gambler, now had himself a horse ranch that kept him free from gunfights and card games. Until Sturvesant of Wells Fargo showed up.

McALLISTER ON THE COMANCHE CROSSING
Matt Chisholm

The Comanche, McAllister owes them a life — and the trail is soaked with the blood of the men who had tried to outrun them before.

QUICK-TRIGGER COUNTRY
Clem Colt

Turkey Red hooked up with Curly Bill Graham's outlaw crew. But wholesale murder was out of Turk's line, so when range war flared he bucked the whole border gang alone . . .

CAMPAIGNING
Jim Miller

Ambushed on the Santa Fe trail, Sean Callahan is saved by two Indian strangers. But there'll be more lead and arrows flying before the band join Kit Carson against the Comanches.

GUNSLINGER'S RANGE
Jackson Cole

Three escaped convicts are out for revenge. They won't rest until they put a bullet through the head of the dirty snake who locked them behind bars.

RUSTLER'S TRAIL
Lee Floren

Jim Carlin knew he would have to stand up and fight because he had staked his claim right in the middle of Big Ike Outland's best grass.

THE TRUTH ABOUT SNAKE RIDGE
Marshall Grover

The troubleshooters came to San Cristobal to help the needy. For Larry and Stretch the turmoil began with a brawl and then an ambush.

WOLF DOG RANGE
Lee Floren

Will Ardery would stop at nothing, unless something stopped him first — like a bullet from Pete Manly's gun.

DEVIL'S DINERO
Marshall Grover

Plagued by remorse, a rich old reprobate hired the Texas Troubleshooters to deliver a fortune in greenbacks to each of his victims.

GUNS OF FURY
Ernest Haycox

Dane Starr, alias Dan Smith, wanted to close the door on his past and hang up his guns, but people wouldn't let him.

DONOVAN
Elmer Kelton

Donovan was supposed to be dead. Uncle Joe Vickers had fired off both barrels of a shotgun into the vicious outlaw's face as he was escaping from jail. Now Uncle Joe had been shot — in just the same way.

CODE OF THE GUN
Gordon D. Shirreffs

MacLean came riding home, with saddle tramp written all over him, but sewn in his shirt-lining was an Arizona Ranger's star.

GAMBLER'S GUN LUCK
Brett Austen

Gamblers seldom live long. Parker was a hell of a gambler. It was his life — or his death . . .

ORPHAN'S PREFERRED
Jim Miller

Sean Callahan answers the call of the Pony Express and fights Indians and outlaws to get the mail through.

DAY OF THE BUZZARD
T. V. Olsen

All Val Penmark cared about was getting the men who killed his wife.

THE MANHUNTER
Gordon D. Shirreffs

Lee Kershaw knew that every Rurale in the territory was on the lookout for him. But the offer of $5,000 in gold to find five small pieces of leather was too good to turn down.

RIFLES ON THE RANGE
Lee Floren

Doc Mike and the farmer stood there alone between Smith and Watson. There was this moment of stillness, and then the roar would start. And somebody would die . . .

HARTIGAN
Marshall Grover

Hartigan had come to Cornerstone to die. He chose the time and the place, and Main Street became a battlefield.

SUNDANCE: OVERKILL
John Benteen

When a wealthy banker's daughter was kidnapped by the Cheyenne, he offered Sundance $10,000 to rescue the girl.